Noelle's Kiss

by

Cindy R. Williams

Christmas Frost, Book 2

Noelle's Kiss

Cover Art by *Debbie Taylor*

The Wild Rose Press, Inc.
PO Box 708
Adams Basin, NY 14410-0708
Visit us at www.thewildrosepress.com

Publishing History
First Sweetheart Rose Edition, 2019
Print ISBN 978-1-5092-2921-5
Digital ISBN 978-1-5092-2922-2

Christmas Frost, Book 2
Published in the United States of America

A shot of energy warmed my cheeks. This was undoubtedly the most incredible physical being I had ever seen, and he was looking at me. I continued to stare back, not knowing what to say, but certainly enjoying the moment, until that annoying college student interrupted my view by handing me my hot chocolate.

"Here you go, miss. That will be four dollars and twenty-five cents, please."

"My treat." Gorgeous Man's low voice had come out of those lips that turned up at the corners, hip still against the counter, his eyes dancing with amusement.

"Oh no, you don't need to pay for mine." I pulled myself together, proud for uttering a complete and coherent sentence.

"I'm happy to do it, Ms. Frost." He pushed his at least six-foot-ten frame away from the counter and winked at me, sending warm honey gliding through my body. Oh, my goodness. He actually winked at me, and it wasn't cheesy. It was absolutely hot. Then a light flashed in my mind. He knew my name.

I took a step back. "Umm...have we met?" Although intrigued, since my divorce I was over cautious where men were concerned.

"CBS 4 Denver, TV reporter Noelle Frost. Everyone in Colorado must know who you are by now."

He had an adorable lopsided grin. I could get used to that. I relaxed a little. I had only worked for the station for a few of months, and it still surprised me when strangers recognized me.

The Christmas Frost Series

FINDING JOY
NOELLE'S KISS
HOLLY'S HEART
CHRISSY'S CATCH

These are the stories of the four Frost sisters, who overcome heartache, betrayal, and ghosts from the past to find true love and bring back the magic of Christmas.

Dedication

To Jeff, my handsome husband,
"You got game!"

Chapter One

Digging around in the purple leather bag I called a purse, I found my wallet at the bottom below my phone, two notebooks, some vanilla lotion, a Polly Pocket, a handful of granola bars, and a bunch of pens and crayons.

"Hot chocolate with caramel—and add a little cinnamon plea—"

I glanced over and up…way up…to see who owned that deep voice coming from the stratosphere who had ordered the same thing I did, almost at the exact same moment.

I zeroed in on the most incredible sea-green eyes shaded by long, black lashes, proving my theory that men get the lashes. After a moment of blatant gawking, I shook my head to release the magnetic hold.

"Uh, yes, we will be taking two hot chocolates with caramel and cinnamon," said the smooth bass voice belonging to those delicious eyes.

"Comin' right up, Sharp Shooter," replied the college student behind the counter.

"No coffee, huh?" was all I could think to ask the extremely tall, extremely well-built man grinning down at me.

"No, I stay away from concentrated caffeine." He crossed his arms and leaned back against the counter, tilting his head to the side to observe me better.

He stayed away from concentrated caffeine. I had no idea what that meant. I heard the words, but my mind was too caught up in the gorgeous specimen standing before me. A shot of energy warmed my cheeks. This was undoubtedly the most incredible physical being I had ever seen, and he was looking at me. I continued to stare back, not knowing what to say, but certainly enjoying the moment, until that annoying college student interrupted my view by handing me my hot chocolate.

"Here you go, miss, that will be four dollars and twenty-five cents please."

"My treat." Gorgeous Man's low voice had come out of those lips that turned up at the corners, hip still against the counter, his eyes dancing with amusement.

"Oh no, you don't need to pay for mine." I pulled myself together, proud for uttering a complete and coherent sentence.

"I'm happy to do it, Ms. Frost." He pushed his at least six-foot-ten frame away from the counter and winked at me, sending warm honey gliding through my body.

Oh, my goodness. He actually winked at me, and it wasn't cheesy. It was absolutely hot. Then a warning light flashed in my mind. He knew my name.

I took a step back. "Umm...have we met?" Although intrigued, since my divorce, I was extra cautious where men were concerned.

"CBS 4 Denver, TV reporter Noelle Frost. Everyone in Colorado must know who you are by now."

He had an adorable lopsided grin. I could get used to that. I relaxed a little. I had only worked for the station for a few of months, and it still surprised me when strangers recognized me.

"Someone pay me already," said the guy behind the counter.

Oh, why didn't Counter Boy stay out of it? I was enjoying this, maybe a little too much.

Green Eyes turned toward the fellow, gave him a twenty, and told him to keep the change.

I stood there longing for the warmth of his eyes to come back to me. Sheesh, I was acting like a teenager crushing on some good-looking guy. My grip on my hot chocolate increased. Stop it, Elle. Shake it off. Get a hold of yourself. Then it dawned on me. This guy seemed familiar, yet I knew if I'd ever met him before I would never have forgotten him. He turned his toned, long and lean body back toward me. My brain did a reboot and I realized who he was.

I managed to get another sentence out of my mouth. "Thanks, Mr. Trayce. I appreciate the hot chocolate." I turned to leave, wishing all the while I could think of something clever or charming to say. "Oh, stop it, Elle. Just go."

Mr. Trayce jumped back. "Stop what?"

Flustered and face flaming, I realized I had blurted that out loud. I gave him my best "I'm really not crazy" smile and choked out, "No, not you, I was talking to myself." I maneuvered quickly out the door with as much dignity as I could muster. I tried to protect my body and my heart by wrapping my wool jacket tight around me against the blast of chilly Colorado wind.

Chapter Two

"I ran into someone today. He has the most gorgeous green eyes." I swished a glob of bubbles with my finger and sank lower in the tub, careful not to let the vanilla-scented froth touch my phone.

"Do tell, Elle." Chrissy laughed at the family rhyme she and my sisters had used on me for years.

"You have to promise not to tell Joy or Holly. I'd never hear the end of it."

"Sure thing—now spill." Chrissy's voice grew more insistent.

Bringing it up may have been a mistake. I didn't want her making too much of this. I was famous for having a brick wall around my heart ever since my divorce four and half years ago. Men were rotten—except my dad, and well, he's not here anymore. A pang of sadness stopped my heart for a moment, as it always did when I thought of my parents and that horrible car crash at Christmas time after my divorce. Somehow the horror of their deaths and my nasty divorce seemed to meld together. What a terrible time it was, and sometimes still is.

"Elle, are you there?" Chrissy's voice brought me back to now.

"Yeah, I'm here. Okay, it's not that big a deal, but it was kind of fun. At least I noticed a man, which is saying a lot for me." Those green eyes appeared in my mind again, and the warmth of the water was not the only thing I felt. The phone slipped and almost fell into the bathtub.

"What was kind of fun? You aren't making any sense." Chrissy's voice grew louder.

"All right, all right, I'll tell you. I stopped at Cuppa Joe's to get my favorite hot chocolate—you know that delicious caramel frappe thing they do? I have them add a little cinnamon. It's so yummy."

"Ugh," she groaned.

I chuckled. "I'm getting to it. So, when I was ordering, this giant man next to me ordered the same thing, even the touch of cinnamon. We practically gave our orders in unison, as if we had rehearsed it. Strange. When I looked at him, I melted. At least six foot ten, dark, glossy hair, filled out his clothes well, and then those eyes. Oh my—those eyes." I stopped there, closed my eyes, and smiled. Those incredible eyes filled my world again.

"Earth to Elle. So, what happened?" the bothersome phone squawked at me.

"Hang on, Chrissy, I was having a memory moment. I mean, how long has it been since I've seen a man like that? Well, never. I met the most gorgeous guy on the planet, and I swear he seemed a little into me, too." I giggled, feeling little butterflies flittering around my stomach.

"Wow. I uh...don't know what to say. If it was anybody else, I'd laugh it off as a joke, but for you, the brick-wall queen, to be struck this hard by a guy—I don't even know what to say."

"He knew my name—said he recognized me from TV. Then I remembered who he was. You won't believe it…Xavier Trayce."

"Triple X? You met Triple X? He's the most eligible bachelor in Colorado—maybe even the entire NBA. Every female who breathes has it bad for him." Chrissy sounded in awe.

I sighed. "I know. It was…well…amazing. Then I blew it. Instead of being all cool and collected, I could hardly speak to him. Plus, I did my usual, you know, 'talk-out-loud-to-myself' thing. He thought I was talking to him. I didn't know what to say then, so naturally I ran out the door."

Silence from the other end of the phone, then laugher rang out.

"It's not funny, Chrissy. My mouth stumbled and froze like a sixteen-year-old talking to the big-shot quarterback in high school. Oh well—at least I won't see him again. Like you said, he's the hottest guy around, and everyone's out to get him." Another deep sigh escaped.

Chrissy's laugh continued.

"It's not that funny," I barked into the phone.

"Why do you always fall for basketball players? I mean, in high school it was yummy Danny McCaffrey; then in college that yucky Blake McNair you married, and now Triple X?" Chrissy had sobered. "But seriously, Elle, you be careful. Triple X is a known ladies' man. After dealing with all the abuse from your creepy ex—you can't go falling for another athlete. They're bad news. I mean, it's time you find someone to love, but not another athlete, p-l-e-a-s-e." I heard the worry in her tone.

"Mommy? I can't sleep," said a small voice from the other side of the bathroom door.

"I'll be out in a minute, sweetie." I pinched out the vanilla candle in the corner of the oversized tub.

"Chrissy, I've got to go. Tatum must've had a bad dream. Besides, I think I've entertained you enough today. Don't worry about me, little sis. I'm not falling for some big basketball player again. Talk to you soon. Love you. Bye."

Chrissy managed to get out, "Love you more," just like our mom.

****

Wrapped in my favorite pink, fuzzy robe, I opened the door to see Tatum curled up in my bed, sound asleep. My heart melted. Smiling, I left the room and made my usual nighttime round of the condo to be sure everything was in its place. I hated to wake up to a messy home. I checked the doors, turned the dishwasher on, got a glass of water, and shut the lights off on my way back upstairs to my bedroom.

After setting the glass on the nightstand, I said a quick prayer and climbed into bed, gently so as not to wake my little angel—my ray of sunshine. I lay on the pillow next to her and brushed back the wisp of hair from her forehead as I whispered, "I can't believe you're already a big kindergartener. You look so tiny. You're the joy in my life, little one."

I leaned over and kissed her soft, warm cheek. She smelled sweet, like berries.

Loving her had gotten me through the awful divorce. I had spent a great deal of time pondering what went wrong and why. He'd changed so much from when we first met. He used to be willing to work together to find happiness. We were a team. Then he became angry all the time. I still didn't understand how in the world he could have become so...cruel. But worse, how could he leave this rosy baby girl?

My stomach tightened as I remembered the anxiety that filled my soul because of baby Tatum's sleep apnea. I had to strap electrical leads around her chest and hook her up to a breathing and heart monitor whenever she slept. So helpless—each nap and night a life and death situation.

Blake didn't seem to understand or even care. He demanded the baby sleep in another room down the hall.

The monitor often malfunctioned. A nervous wreck, I crept out of bed each night and curled up on Tatum's floor with my hand reaching up into the crib, touching the side of her chest. I still woke up with nightmares full of his piercing voice berating me in the middle of the night as he yanked me off the floor shouting, "Leave her be. Get back in here with me. That is your place, woman."

Not tonight. No...not tonight. I pushed the nightmare away, not allowing myself to think about the rest of it. I had to banish that recurring nightmare. Blake is out of our lives. He can't hurt us anymore.

I mentally switched gears and focused on the memory of those green eyes smiling down at me from that lovely specimen of a man. My stomach settled down. Triple X—what a silly nickname for a basketball player. I know it's because he tends to get more than his fair share of triple doubles in games, but Triple X, really? Maybe it's also a play on his unusual first name, Xavier.

I snuggled in closer to Tatum and smiled as I drifted off to sleep. The last thing I remembered was hoping that tonight I would get a good night's rest with those green eyes smiling at me in my dreams, keeping that dreadful former marriage nightmare at bay.

Chapter Three

I woke up agitated, my mind full of images of that awful dream. Images of baby Tatum hooked to her monitor, crying as the alarm blared. Waves of panic smothering me as Blake held me down, preventing me from getting to her as he yelled, "You. Stupid Woman. Get that yapping baby to shut up."

Then it flashed to Blake and a co-worker, Cherise, his umm, mistress, for want of a better title, together in our hot tub—appearing as one single silhouette framed by the moonlight.

Always the same nightmare—started and ended the same. It made me so sick, my stomach ached.

Once again, I thought about Blake's terrible temper and how he'd treated me. I had protected Tatum from his angry outbursts, but worried constantly that she and I would do something to set him off. Abusers blame their victims and don't accept responsibility for their own actions. I rubbed my stomach, reminding myself that it was over. Tatum and I were safe, at least for now.

Maybe the fact that he still had visitation rights and could exercise them at any time was what kept that ugly nightmare alive.

Eventually, Blake was mostly out of our lives. He had only arranged to see Tatum a few times before he'd moved to California. He had proudly informed me that he was living with a starlet and too busy to be bothered with a little brat.

I was thrilled. I didn't want Tatum around him. I had worried about his horrid temper and didn't want her subjected to it. He was certainly not the man I thought I'd married. I had to get over my past. I had to move on and let it go. I took a long, slow, deep breath and felt my stomach settling down.

I never talked about my recurring nightmare with my sisters. They would sympathize with me, but I was sure they would also insist I see a shrink to make it go away. Maybe I should.

Tatum still slept, so I rolled over to watch her. What an angel and a blessing. Matching my breathing to hers, I dozed off into a peaceful sleep until her little arm bonked me in the nose as she stretched herself awake.

"Hey, baby girl, watch the arm. Are you going to grow up to be a boxer?" I teased her.

"No, Mommy, I'm going to be a gymnaster." She scrunched her nose at me.

"A gymnast." I grinned at her as I tapped the end of her cute little nose.

"That's what I said, a gymnaster." She jutted her chin out. Oh my. We Frost women were known for being stubborn. My little darling had it in spades. I gave her a big hug.

"Okay. Let's get up and make the bed, get dressed, and…" I glanced at the clock. "Ah—oh. We need to leave in fifteen minutes to get to 'gymnaster' class."

****

Tatum and I held hands as we skipped down the hall in the Olympic Training Facility.

"Mommy, look at that man. He's as tall as a tree." Tatum pointed.

"It's not nice to point," I reminded her, then caught my breath. It was the basketball player with those incredible green eyes and lopsided grin.

"But it's true." Tatum smiled up at me.

"Hello, Ms. Frost. It's good to see you again," said the tree.

"Hello, Mr. Trayce." I smiled.

"It's Xavier. But please, call me Zave."

"Zave?" I tilted my head as I looked up at the good-looking man.

"Yes. Z-a-v-e, rhymes with Dave. I know it's not an X, but it works. I've always wished we wrote phonetically, especially with a name like mine." He smiled at me.

A little frog bounced around in my stomach. I really liked that smile. He sure looked delicious for so early on a Saturday morning.

"Mommy, I'm gonna be late." Tatum tugged on my arm.

"Well, hello, little one. Do you belong to this lovely lady?" Zave knelt on one knee, then lowered himself all the way down to Tatum's eye level, which was quite a feat to watch.

"Yes, I'm her *big* girl. I'm a gymnaster. Are you a giant?"

I couldn't stop a chuckle from escaping my lips but rallied fast. "No, honey, Zave is not a giant. He's a basketball player."

"Oh, that is a good thing for giants to do. Are you any good?" Tatum asked without missing a beat.

"Well, I do know how to run up and down the

basketball court, and I try my best to put that pesky orange ball in the hoop. How about you? Are you a good gymnaster?" Zave remained squatting down as he spoke to Tatum.

"Uh huh. I can do flipper-doodles." She grinned, eyes sparkling.

"Well, then you really are a gymnaster. Would you and your mommy like to have some ice cream with me today after your class?" Zave smiled at Tatum and then looked up at me.

The sunlight from the wall of windows in the hallway flashed in those green eyes, making them as brilliant as an ocean along a white, sandy beach in some travel brochure. My heart sped up as if it were a running wheel for a little chipmunk.

"Can we, Mommy?" Tatum tugged my hand.

"Can we what?" I'd lost all train of thought in those eyes.

Zave rose to a standing position, that big lopsided grin splitting his cheeks. "Ice cream. May I buy you two some ice cream today?"

"Please, please. Can we have some ice cream with Tree?" Tatum tugged at my hand.

"Tatum…Zave is not a tree or a giant." My cheeks warmed.

Zave laughed a full belly laugh. Soon Tatum and I joined him.

"There you are, Triple X. I've been looking all over for you, baby. You're taking me to lunch today." A tall, scantily dressed, high-heeled, fluffy-ginger-haired girl sidled up to Zave.

My heart dropped. The woman looked as if she'd stepped out of a magazine.

All laughter stopped. Zave's face turned bright red. I had no idea trees could turn red.

"Uh…" he stumbled.

"No worries. We have plans today. It was good to see you. Come on, sweetie, time for class." I pulled Tatum down the hall as quickly as possible, her little legs almost running. My stomach hurt—or was it my heart? I'd only seen this guy two times. Forget him.

I pulled Tatum out of her class a few minutes early, and we exited through a side door. I wanted to leave quickly, in case Zave was waiting for us in the hall. He's a player, I decided, and I don't need any more players.

Chapter Four

"Hi, Joy." I dropped a bright pink tote bag with some things Tatum might need for the afternoon on a chair in Joy's kitchen.

"Aunt Elle." Three hooligans attacked me from behind, almost knocking me down.

"What are you guys, ninjas or something?" I turned around to give my nephews a group hug. They laughed and ran back out of the room, Tatum chasing after them.

"Thanks for watching Tatum, sis. Until I get a little seniority, I'm stuck working the Saturday shift."

"I'm happy to do it. Tatum is easy compared to the boys. Besides they seem to behave better when she's here." She looked back at me and grinned. "My hoodlums made a fort out of blankets and boxes in the family room. I promised them they could eat pizza and watch *Scooby Doo*." Joy dried her hands on a towel and leaned over to give me a hug.

"I should be home shortly after the six o'clock broadcast. I really do appreciate you. I don't know what I'd have done without you to tend Tatum so I could go back to work after the divorce, and Mom and Dad..." We both teared up a little. "It's still so hard, isn't it?" I said with a lump in my throat.

"Yes, I miss them every day. I wish they were here to be a part of our children's lives." Joy straightened

15

her shoulders and added, "Well it's up to us to make sure we share plenty of stories about them with the kids, so they'll know them in their hearts."

"Right..." I gave her a sad smile, then glanced around the large, warm, and tidy kitchen. I was glad Joy and her kids lived in our childhood home. It made the most sense for them to be there. I noticed the time on our mother's old, kitschy, tail-twitching, round-eyed black-cat clock.

"I've got to run. I have a story at the Rose Conservatory today. It's soft news—no shooting, death, fighting, or anything—just a nice story about people doing something good for the community. See you, and thanks again, sis." I hugged her quick, called out, "Bye. Tatum," and hurried out the door.

****

"Thank you, Dr. Rasmussen. That was a lovely story. One of the more pleasant ones I've been asked to cover." I shook his hand.

"Ronald, please call me Ronald. My doctorate is a PhD, and unless you are one of my students at Pikes Peak Community College, no need to include my title before my name." Not letting go of my hand, he continued. "I am glad you mentioned that your favorite roses were the pink mini-roses. Many scholars in the scientific community ignore them. You see, miniature roses are nothing more than hybrids, accentuating small blooms, which is a major fault in roses. Not many inside the community see beauty in their failure." The man looked at me through smudged, round spectacles.

Oops, I didn't know mini roses were frowned upon by rose experts. "I think they're lovely," I said quietly, not wanting to start a debate.

"Yes, you said that when talking to me on the camera...well...even so, I believe I would like to invite you to accompany me to my lecture Thursday night in the Rose Auditorium here on campus. As a renowned authority in the American Rose Society on the Rosa Glauea, or Red Leaf Rose, I have been asked to speak on its success in producing wide hips on its flower in its second bloom." He lowered his chin and peered at me above his glasses. "It should prove extremely interesting. Rosa Glauea has a low sucker rate, making it such a titillating subject to cover. As a matter of fact, it reminds me of you." He squeezed my hand as if to make his point.

I pulled my hand away gently from his clammy one. Oh no, I groaned inwardly. Dr. Rasmussen seemed like a nice man, but he wasn't my type. Plus, I think he just told me I have wide hips. Other than that, the man had brains but lacked the self-awareness that he might be overzealous in his field—or umm, boring. Sure, he was tall, but it was that awkward tall, as if he shot up too fast when he was a teenager and never outgrew that gangly stage. His clothes hung off his bony shoulders like a sack on a coat rack.

That wasn't so bad, but his breath smelled like day-old fish. When I interviewed him on camera, he had a way of squinting one eye as he looked at me as if he were examining one of his precious roses and looking for aphids. I guess he decided I wasn't a host for bugs after all.

"Noelle—I may call you Noelle, may I not? About Thursday?" He actually tapped his foot a few times.

Zave's image flitted through my mind. Dr. Rasmussen was nothing like him. Maybe Chrissy was right. Maybe I ought to try going out with someone completely different. I heard myself say, "Certainly, Dr. Rasmu—Ronald. I would enjoy attending your lecture."

The man grasped my hand once again. "It starts at seven p.m. sharp. Please arrive a half hour early. I'd like to introduce you to some of the top roseologists in the country. I do believe you will find it an honor being on my arm. I'm sure you will know to dress scholarly, not like a television personage." He turned his squint on my attire and frowned. "A black dress with pearls would be most appropriate." He looked at my feet and added, "None of those high-heeled shoes. Sensible flats would be best."

Oh my, I wondered, what had I gotten myself into? This guy couldn't be for real. Stop it. Give him a chance. I might as well check out his world. At least it would get my sisters off my back. I disengaged my hand from his surprisingly strong hold and nodded my head to Freddy, my favorite camera man. It was time to go.

"Thank you again, Dr.—Ronald. I will be prompt Thursday, and yes, I have a black dress and pearls." I stopped talking before any negative thoughts going through my head jumped out. I dreaded this upcoming date, my attitude already on the sour side of anticipation.

****

"Mommy, we saw you on TV tonight. You looked so pretty. Can we go see the roses?" Tatum ran at me with her arms opened wide.

My heart swelled as I picked her up and gave her a big squeeze, smelling the soft scent of vanilla shampoo. My back gave a tweak. My little angel was getting too heavy to sweep up into my arms like this.

"You want to see the roses? Sure, sweetie. One evening this week. What did you and your ninja cousins do today?"

"We fought the black zoodah." Her little heart-shaped face looked so serious.

"The what?"

"The black zoodah. It's a giant Gila monster. If it bites you, it never lets go."

"Charlie brought a book home from the school library on Gila monsters. He was thrilled to death to scare his little brothers with it—Tatum, too." Joy came into the kitchen and poured herself a glass of water. "You two want to stay for dinner? Tuna casserole's in the oven."

Out of the corner of my eye, I noticed Tatum's nose scrunch.

"Thanks, sis, but no thanks. I think I'll take Tatum out for a burger tonight. Are you game, little gymnaster?"

"Sure." She patted my cheeks, and I set her down and took her hand.

"Before you go, I want to ask you what is going on in your love life. Any dates?" Joy had her hands on her hips in a big-sister stance.

"As a matter of fact, I have a date this Thursday night with Dr. Rasmussen, the rose specialist I did the interview with today. Can Tatum stay with you and the boys from six twenty until around ten that evening?" I watched as Joy's mouth fell open. I laughed. I hadn't had a date in at least six months, and she knew it. All my sisters kept up on each other's dating lives. We were nosy that way.

"He isn't your usual…uh…jock?" She frowned.

Tatum wrinkled her nose again. "Does that mean he's gonna be my new daddy?"

Stunned, I said, "No, of course not. It means that I will go listen to him talk, then come right back home. He's just a friend. You know, like Hunter is your friend at school."

"Oh, Hunter's my boyfriend. We're going to get married when we're eight and have five children." Tatum's eyes lit up.

"Is that right?" I bit my lip.

She nodded her head and grinned as if it were so because she said so.

Oh, the optimism of youth.

"Yup. But, Mommy, how 'bout you marry Tree Man? I liked him. He can be my daddy."

Joy interjected, "Who is Tree Man?"

I froze. No, this couldn't be. I wasn't ready to talk about Zave to anyone, but Chrissy. Besides, there really wasn't anything to say. I looked from Tatum to Joy.

Tatum offered her five-year-old wisdom. "He's a giant. We were supposed to eat ice cream, but we snucked out." She leaned toward Joy like she was going to share a secret and added, "I don't think he likes that other lady. I think he likes Mommy."

"Noelle Belle Frost, what is she talking about?" Joy's hands were in fists this time when she placed them on her hips.

Darn, I had to clear this up. "Nothing. Nothing, really. I ran into Zave, I mean Xavier Trayce, the Denver Nuggets basketball player, last week. Then Tatum and I saw him again at the Olympic Training Facility before her gymnastics class this morning. I guess he made a good impression on her." I looked Joy straight in the eyes, hoping she couldn't read the hope and then disappointment in my own.

After a moment she dropped her hands to her sides and said, "Okay, then. If any more exciting man-sightings happen to you, I want to know about it. You hear?"

"Yes, bossy big sister," I said, then sighed with relief. I gave Joy a quick hug. "Thanks again, sis. See you Thursday evening. Let's go, my tattletale little angel." I grabbed Tatum's hand and her tote bag and escaped before my sister thought up any more questions.

Chapter Five

It seemed that when you dreaded something, it came even faster. I couldn't believe I'd committed to go to a lecture on roses with Dr. Rasmussen. I had sure set myself up for a dull night. I dropped Tatum off to play with the Ninja Warriors and then spent the rest of the driving time giving myself a pep talk. "Come on, Elle, give it a chance. You might be surprised. Attitude is everything. Dr. Rasmussen might turn out to be the guy of your dreams."

My deep inner, hopeful self voiced this aloud to my outer skeptical ears. The image of a tree of a man with striking green eyes flashed in my mind. I scolded myself and pushed it away. I wasn't really ready for a man in my life anyway. "Men aren't trustworthy," I told that bothersome voice.

"Time to get out, Elle. This could be a great evening." My rah-rah talk got me out of the car. I adjusted my black dress and pearls, which I would have worn even if the good doctor hadn't suggested it. I grinned and glanced at my heels. "Nope, Dr. Rasmussen, I won't be ordered around ever again by any man."

I forced myself to walk into the auditorium with quiet dignity. Dr. Rasmussen was standing on the stage, visiting with some dusty-looking older gentlemen. I walked to the front and waited within his line of sight.

Compared to Zave, the man was not much of a looker. "Oh, just stop it right now, Elle." It was a good thing I was too far away for the doctor to hear my outburst.

"Noelle. Please come and join us. I would like you to meet my distinguished colleagues." The doctor bounced on the balls of his feet in what might have been excitement.

I took the stairs near them. As I approached, I found myself moving slower and slower. "Just go." I scolded myself.

"I beg your pardon?" the doctor said.

I must have turned red. I really need to get control of my "speaking-to-myself-out-loud" thing. "Oh, I'm sorry; did I say that out loud?"

The small group stared at me. Awkward.

"Hello, I'm Noelle Frost." I pasted on my most brilliant TV-reporter smile.

Dr. Rasmussen kicked into gear with introductions of doctor of this, expert of that, and presidents of local Rose Society chapters. One mousy little lady glared hard at me, then turned her back and stepped closer to Dr. Rasmussen.

Oh, she must be enamored with him. Now there was something I could focus on tonight. I'd see if I could help two nice people get together. They seemed to be a perfect match.

After the introductions, the various "rose people" ignored me and shared "rose talk." I was totally out of my element; other than color and their lovely scent, I was lost. I slipped away and found a seat on the second row near the end.

The lecture turned out as I feared—dry, drier, and

driest. I dozed off several times, awaking periodically to eyes boring into me. The little mousy lady could do the "dagger eyes" with perfection.

Afterward at the small reception for the elite in the field of roses, Dr. Rasmussen pulled me to his side and plopped his arm over my shoulder.

He proceeded to lean on me—an uncomfortable stance to be sure, with my black heels making me almost as tall as him. Plus, I didn't know this man well enough to become his leaning post as he drank a few cocktails.

"Did you enjoy my lecture?" he asked with a slight slur. I found the smell of alcohol mixed with day-old fish staggering.

"This is not going to work out." Once again, I said this out loud.

"What was that?" The tipsy man's eyes grew large.

"Uh…you must work out." I moved out from under his arm and turned him to face the side of the room. "See Dr. Sands, that pretty little lady in the brown shrug over there? She has been watching you most of the night. I think she is fascinated with your lecture and…with you." He looked over at her, then back at me. He had a cockeyed grin. He must not be much of a drinker.

"Come on, Dr. Rasmussen…"

"Call me Ronald."

"Come on, Ronald. It's time to meet your destiny."

****

"Thanks, sis," I whispered as I carried my sleeping angel out to the car.

"How did it go?" Joy asked. I could hear the hope in her voice.

"You know, it actually went well for Dr. Rasmussen and Dr. Sands. I think there may be wedding bells in their future."

"What?" She sounded thoroughly confused.

I smiled. "Let's say he wasn't my type, so I played matchmaker." I wrapped the seatbelt around Tatum and snapped it. She sighed but remained asleep. "Thank you, Joy. What would I do without you?" I gave her a big hug and hopped into the car. "Since it's not a Mason Jar Night for us Friday, do you and the boys want to come over for popcorn and a ninja movie?"

"Sure. The boys will love it."

"So will Tatum. Night, love you."

"Love you more."

Chapter Six

"Ah, Friday again, my last day of the week in Denver," I said to no one in particular. I actually enjoyed life as a TV reporter. Monday through Friday, I drove to Denver to cover stories there. On Saturdays, I was expected to sniff out happenings in Colorado Springs, where I lived. I usually did research and taped a story each day except Sunday. My schedule worked out well for a single parent.

My latest story on a local infestation of Africanized bees was in the can early—luckily without me and my favorite cameraman, Freddy, getting stung. I made some calls to organize tomorrow's shoot, then left for the hour-long drive to Colorado Springs. The early afternoon crisp air and bright sunshine added to my good mood. Great, I would make it in time to get Tatum from all-day kindergarten. I loved it when I could leave work early enough to pick her up. That gave us an early start on weekend fun. I gave Joy a quick call to let her know she didn't need to pick her up today when she picked up Charlie.

Tatum ran to me, grabbed my arm, and held on tight.

"Hello, little missy. What wonderful things did you learn today?" I pulled her close and gave her a hug.

"I learnded that you ruined my life." Tears filled her eyes.

"What? How in the world did I ruin your life?" That certainly wasn't what I'd expected to hear.

"Well, today when me and Cassidy went to recess, she let me wear one of her shoes, so I let her wear one of mine—but it felt weird 'cause her shoe is bigger than mine, and it flew off when I chased Hunter. Then Hunter said him and his dad—you know he doesn't have a mama—saw you on TV talking about roses."

She stopped and looked at me as if she expected me to understand.

"O…kay…but how did that ruin your life?"

"Because, Mommy—" She stamped her foot. "—his dad said you were as pretty as the roses, and Hunter said his dad is always right, so now he is going to marry you when he turns eight, unless his dad does." Her voice changed to pleading. "Please marry his dad so I can marry Hunter."

"Honey, I promise I won't marry Hunter. He's all yours. Besides, I thought you wanted me to marry the tree man." I smiled as I pulled her back into another big hug.

She gave me a big squeeze back. "I do."

"I can't marry Hunter's dad and the tree man. In fact, I'm not planning on marrying anyone. It's you and me, kiddo."

She smiled and hopped into the car. "Where are we going?"

Wow, that was an easy fix. I wish my grown-up problems were that easy to resolve. I clicked my seat belt, then said, "To the store to get some groceries and some things for our movie night with your Ninja Warrior cousins."

"Yay!"

****

Saturday and Sunday were quiet days for Tatum and me. Gymnastics for her; then I dropped her off at Joy's while I taped a local story. Later, we played dress-up and restaurant. Tatum "cooked" our dinner—cereal and bananas and milk, sprinkled with chocolate chips. Afterward, we read books on the couch, then searched for places we could go on vacation when school was out next summer. On Sunday, we attended church and had a quiet lunch and a delicious nap on my bed. I loved our weekends together. How blessed I was to have this little girl in my life. I often reminded myself that I didn't need a man to make me happy. I had my little corner of Heaven on Earth right here. In fact, the nightmares that weekend seemed to be a little less powerful.

****

I sat at my desk at CBS 4 Denver's Colorado Springs office on Monday morning. The usual racket surrounded me in the noisy open room called the bullpen. I tried to get my head around possible story ideas for the week. Nothing new jumped out at me.

"Okay, time to get busy, Elle." This time I purposely spoke out loud to give myself a little kick in the pants. I gave up brainstorming and focused on the shoot I had in about an hour at a local shopping center, preparing to host a Thanksgiving reenactment and fundraiser next month. Not a hot story, but that's what you got on a slow day.

"Elle, these here itty-bitty roses just arrived."

I looked up to see lovely miniature pink roses in a crystal vase. "Thank you, Julie. Who are they from?"

"I don't know. I think there's a card here

somewhere." The receptionist turned the flowers around until a little robin's-egg-blue envelope faced me. She set the flowers on my desk and waited with excitement.

I had learned quickly that Julie was kind of a mother figure here, and the office gossip. She knew everyone's business, but she had a big heart.

I gulped, afraid they were from the rose professor, then opened the card and read it silently.

Dear Ms. Frost,

I would like the opportunity to make up for the ice cream owed to you and Miss Tatum. Would you be so kind as to let me know if there is an evening this week that would be convenient other than game nights, Tuesday, Thursday, and Friday? Which leaves only today or Wednesday. Sorry.

I know you are busy with your work and these are school nights for the little lady, so I promise we would only be an hour.

Please say yes and respond by text to 720-255-1360.

The Tree

P.S. I saw your report on the pink mini roses. You looked lovely, by the way.

My heart did a little skip. I set the card on my desk. Did the guy actually mean it? I was surprised he even remembered us. I mean, I'm sure he has a harem of ladies hanging all over him. "You only saw one girl, Elle," I scolded myself out loud.

"Who did you see, and who is the Tree?" Julie asked. She had sidled around my desk and read over my shoulder.

I had forgotten she was there. "Umm...nobody,

and he is just a guy, a super-tall guy. My little girl called him Tree. You know kids, they say it as they see it. We ran into him at the Olympic Training Facility where I take Tatum for gymnastics." I realized I was rambling and anything I told her was bound to be water cooler news by the end of the day. I dropped the card into my purple bag.

Julie turned to leave, then paused and leaned toward me with a serious look on her face. "You know, Elle, I'm always one to mind my own business, but I would be careful if I were you. This fellow takes his games pretty seriously. And his lady friends not seriously at all. Sounds like one of those wastrels that has to be at the bar three times a week to watch them sports games with his buddies. These little flowers are lovely and all, but you best be guarding your heart."

I sat at my desk, fighting a smile. For a man I'd run into at Cuppa Joe's, he sure had many titles—Triple X, Sharpshooter, Xavier Trayce, Zave, Man-With-a-Harem, Tree, and now Wastrel. Which was the real man? Always one for a good mystery, I decided I'd take him up on his ice cream offer on Wednesday and sent him a quick text. This may make a good story for that novel I hope to write someday.

Chapter Seven

I was in a hurry when I picked up Tatum late afternoon Wednesday from Joy's.

"We already ate, sis. Mac and cheese was the unanimous choice of the wild ninjas tonight." Joy brushed the hair from her forehead and plopped into a kitchen chair.

I grabbed Tatum's jacket and backpack. "Thanks, Joy. You're the best." I leaned over and gave her a quick kiss on the cheek. "See you tomorrow." I scooted my daughter toward the door. I wanted to get to Josh & John's Ice Cream a little early so I could watch Zave come in. Not sure why.

I'd dressed up for work with tonight in mind. I had on my favorite teal blouse. I knew the color brought out the green and blue in my hazel eyes. I loved the way my black skirt with the pleats around the left knee made me look slim, or at least I thought it did. My three-inch black pumps brought me close to six feet tall, but I'd never have to worry about heels with this guy. I had added a twenty-inch gold chain with obsidian beads every few inches and matching dangling earrings. I flattered myself that the gold brought out the golden highlights in my dark blond hair. I wanted to look good this evening, even though it was a casual ice cream date.

"Where're we going, Mommy?"

I hadn't told Tatum about tonight because I knew she'd tell Joy. I wasn't ready to share anything more about Zave with my sisters yet. Stop kidding yourself, I scolded myself. There was nothing to share. A ripple buzzed through my chest, calling me a liar.

"We are going for ice cream with the tall man you call Tree." I couldn't keep the smile from breaking out.

"Yay! Tree man. Tree man." She clapped her hands together several times in delight.

Well, that was a good sign. She already liked Zave. I'd never let other men meet her before. Plus, including last week's boring rose lecture, I had only been on a handful of dates since the divorce. I knew I was afraid to trust a man again, afraid to trust my own judgement where they were concerned. This was a big step for both of us.

It's only ice cream, I said to myself to calm my racing heartbeat. Who was I kidding? In my heart I knew I hoped for more.

I turned on Tatum's favorite Disney music CD, and we sang along. A few minutes later, my mind started to wander, and a red flag popped up, causing lightning bugs to bounce around in my stomach, warning me that this could be a big mistake.

Zave was an athlete, like my ex-husband. I'd known Blake for two semesters at college before we married. He was handsome, driven, and pursued me with a passion. It was flattering. During that time, he was extremely busy with basketball and his classes. I stayed busy, too, with my upper-level courses for my degree in communications and broadcasting and doing an internship as a weather girl for the local station. In hindsight, we hadn't spent that much time together, and

I really didn't know him well.

I thought Blake was great at first, but then after we married his true nature surfaced. I soon realized that when we were dating, the times he was quiet, when I thought he was a deep thinker, in reality he was holding tight to his temper. It became evident he wanted a compliant, slave-like wife he could control.

I pushed those thoughts away, telling myself that I wasn't the same young naive college girl. I was stronger now. Zave was not Blake. Zave seemed to be a good guy, and I thought I might be ready to pry my heart open again. I needed to give him the benefit of the doubt, give this a chance. Besides, it was just ice cream. My stomach swirled again, warning me to be careful.

"There's the ice cream store, Mommy." Tatum interrupted my thoughts.

"Good eyes, little lady."

Since it was dinner time, there were only a few people there. Good. Decorated in a variety of pastels, the entire store seemed built to make people smile. Purple appeared to be the predominant color. One wall was old brick. Paper lanterns glowed from the ceiling— a real warm, fuzzy place.

I spied a table in the far corner and headed over while Tatum ran to the glass serving area to ogle the flavors. The door opened, and Zave stepped in. My heart stopped. Not skipped a beat—flat out stopped.

He didn't see me at first. It gave me a moment to study him—and catch my breath. Absolutely gorgeous human being, that man. Those brilliant green eyes that had haunted me, now seemed moss colored from far away. His dark hair looked like he'd raked his fingers through it; some of it stood on end—adorable. The corners of his mouth turned up when he saw Tatum at the ice cream counter. Sure he looked great, but he was just a guy, and I was just checking things out. I wasn't going to do something dumb again, I cautioned myself as I sat frozen to the bench, heart pounding.

He had to be the best-looking guy on the planet.

He looked around the ice cream parlor, and our eyes met. A devilish grin appeared and grew slowly until it lit up his entire face.

If I hadn't already been sitting down, I'm afraid I would have swooned like one of those damsels in distress in a romance novel. "Come on, Elle, it's ice cream…just ice cream," I scolded myself out loud.

He walked toward me with the grace of an athlete. Even his walk was sexy. I couldn't take my eyes off him. He reached the table, still smiling. I had no idea if I was smiling or if my mouth was hanging open like a big-mouth frog.

"Hello, Noelle," he said in a deep, smooth-as-honey voice that warmed my soul.

"Hi," I managed to croak.

His eyes seemed to smolder as he continued to look at me. I knew mine had absolutely melted into his.

"Thank you for meeting me here tonight. I was worried you wouldn't after Rhonda did her clinging act." Zave shuffled his feet like a little boy, embarrassed and worried.

This guy was too cute.

"Rhonda, huh? She seemed pretty friendly, like you and she were…umm, together." I closed my mouth tight. Sheesh—as if I had some claim on the man.

"She's the daughter of the team owner and runs through the players like…" He bit his lower lip as if he didn't want to say something rude about her. "I guess I'm her latest target, but trust me when I tell you, I'm not and will never become involved with Rhonda Santori." Zave's smile had turned into a straight line. He looked sincere. "She's a sweet girl but needs something to occupy her time, and that something isn't going to be me."

"Good," I said. "I mean...well, it's good to see you. Great, Elle, smooth, really smooth."

"Pardon me?" The man's eyebrows pinched in the center.

"Oh, um, did I say that out loud?" I wrung my hands on my lap. I couldn't believe I let that slip out in front of this handsome creature.

He grinned and asked, "May I?" as he motioned toward the booth.

"Oh, sure." My bag was next to me, so he had to sit across the table. I knew I was putting up a physical barrier, but I had to protect my heart.

"I'm happy to see you. I've been thinking about you and your charming little girl. Wednesday seemed like a year away. I doubled my regular daily free throws to pass the time." Zave grinned that lopsided little-boy grin.

My busy little butterflies took a spin around my insides. "Settle down," I scolded them.

"What?" he asked as he leaned his head toward me as if to hear me better.

"Uh, I was saying that I guess when your free throw percentage jumps a few points, you have us Frost girls to thank." I flashed my TV smile and saw him take a slow, deep breath. I increased my smile so my dimples showed.

He caught his breath and his eyes widened.

"So, you get butterflies, too," I spilled out. I slapped my hand over my mouth, mortified. Why, oh why, did I say that out loud?

The spell was broken, and Zave let out that belly laugh that was so contagious I laughed along with him. We settled back down, and I checked on Tatum. She looked mesmerized by the long row of mix-ins.

"You know, Noelle, you're a topic of discussion among the team lately." He tilted his head to the side and watched me.

"What do you mean?" I straightened my back.

"Some of the guys say they watch the news now just to see you. I have to admit, it's my fault. Whenever there's a TV around in a locker room, I turn on the news to catch your report, and the guys can't help but notice you. You're one lovely lady." He leaned back in his seat and watched me with a soft smile.

I opened my mouth to say something, but nothing came to mind, so I closed it. As I did, his eyes left mine and looked at my lips. Flutterbies, I mean butterflies, flew frantically in my stomach as heat coursed through me. I couldn't help but answer his probing gaze with a slow smile of my own.

His hand reached out toward mine. I watched as he ran a long, calloused finger up my pointer finger, then continued across my hand and down my baby finger.

An electrical current shot through me and I jumped up. This was all too fast for me. "Uh, I think Tatum needs me."

Zave stood up as well and followed me. A lady stepped between us and asked him for an autograph. I continued walking to the counter. Tatum had asked

"Jenn," so the name tag said, for a taste of "pink" ice cream and licked the tiny sample spoon.

I tilted my head to hear the exchange between the lady and Zave.

"You're my oldest son's favorite player, and his birthday's Friday." She held out a napkin and a pen. Two little boys stood next to her. Both of them had their mouths open in awe, heads tilted way back as if looking up at a skyscraper.

"Sure. What's his name?" Zave took the pen and paper. She told him, and Zave stepped over to the counter and spoke out loud as he wrote, "To Cole, Happy Birthday, and always be good to your mother. Triple X." He handed it back to her, then looked at the two little boys, blinked at them, and said, "Hi, guys." They shrieked with laughter and ran to the other end of the ice cream counter.

"Sorry about that, Mr. Trayce. My little boys are…um…have never seen anyone as big as you." She frowned and added, "Oh, that might not have been a very nice thing to say."

"'Tis only true, madam. My own dear mother tells me I'm quite a tall drink of water. Tell your son I'll make a free throw in the next game for him."

"Thanks." She grinned and joined her youngsters.

"That was nice of you." I placed my hand on his arm. Muscles moved under my fingers. My fingers tingled. Wow! His arm was ripped.

"I'm a nice guy, Noelle. Stick around, you'll see." His eyes crinkled and the corners of his lips turned up. "I don't mean to scare you, but I know you feel it, too. There's something between us, and I would like to find out what." He took my hand from his arm and held it.

Those annoying butterflies zipped another lap around my midsection. This time I didn't jump like a scared rabbit.

Chapter Eight

"Bubble gum, I want bubble gum ice cream with gummy bears and sprinkles. Please, Mommy?" Tatum danced up and down.

"Sure, sweetie, but first, please say 'Hi' to Mr. Trayce." I stood between her and Zave, so I stepped back so she could see him.

Zave let go of my hand and held his out as he bent forward to shake Tatum's. "Hi, Tatum. Please call me Zave, or Tree is fine, too." Zave winked at me.

Even his wink was enough to make the butterflies stir again. Oh boy, I need to be careful with this one.

"Hi, Tree. I told Mommy she has to marry you or Hunter's daddy, so Hunter won't. Hunter's daddy watches Mommy on TV, you know, and thinks she's really pretty." She paused long enough to take a much-needed breath.

I glanced up at Zave. His eyes were wide with astonishment.

"See, me and Hunter are getting married when we're eight. So, you don't have to marry my mommy, but it's okay if you do. Mommy said you have 'gorgeous green eyes.'" She giggled before adding, "I think that means she loves you. I don't mind having a giant for a daddy." Tatum nodded her head at both of us as if she had just explained how the world rotates, and so now we could all get our ice cream.

Oh my...extremely awkward. Heat radiated from every pore in my face. As nice a guy as he seemed to be, if I were Zave, that little speech would have scared me to death. I would sneak—no, run—out of the ice cream shop as fast as I could. I felt like a silly teenager when your girlfriend tells the guy you like that you like him. On second thought, I decided maybe this was a good test. Tatum and I were an incredibly wonderful package deal—if he couldn't handle the two of us, then too bad for him. I didn't trust men, anyway, and especially athletes—and he was both. Let's see what this guy was made of.

I focused on helping Tatum order, and then chose a new flavor, spicy chocolate with jalapeno peppers. My sister, Holly, had mentioned it, and my mouth had watered ever since. Sounded a bit strange, but she said it gave an incredible twist to the rich chocolate. It was a night for trying new things. The lady at the counter handed me the cone, and I took a small lick. Oh...my...goodness. The chocolate tasted rich, and after I swallowed it, a slight warm burn hit my mouth. It was divine—unique, but divine. I guess it was true that chocolate soothed whatever ailed you—even spicy chocolate.

Zave chose a triple decker with a scoop of vanilla, chocolate, and strawberry.

"You're a classical ice cream eater, aren't you?" I smiled at him.

"Yup. Sometimes basics are the best." He took a taste off the top scoop.

"That will be nineteen dollars and fifty-six cents, please." The employee at the counter, dressed in various shades of purple, smiled up at us.

My purse sat across the room, still at the table. I turned to get it, and there was Zave, standing so close that I spun right into his arms. The world stopped. I didn't dare look up at him, unsure if I wanted to, unsure if I was ready to hear what he had to say.

"Noelle, look at me," Zave said quietly.

His voice, so deep and soft above my ear, caused a shiver throughout my body. I tried to shake it off. I didn't know if I could look at those green eyes and not fall apart. I mean, I'd met the guy a few weeks ago, and had only seen him three times, but somehow what he thought mattered to me.

"Noelle, please look at me," Zave repeated in almost a whisper.

My heart gave one final punch. Still in his arms, I tilted my head and met his crystal-clear emerald eyes.

"Please listen carefully. Don't run away. I think you may have been hurt in the past, but I'm not that man. I'm beginning to see that the Frost women, young and old, speak their minds." His eyes crinkled, then he continued, "Yes, what Tatum said took me back for a moment."

I stiffened in his arms.

"We have some pretty strong chemistry going on between us, and you've felt it, too. I know, because you blurted out something about little butterflies in your stomach when we were at the table." He paused. The corner of his mouth twitched, then he added, "What Tatum said made me realize that even a five-year-old, a brilliant five-year-old, can see that there's something special going on here. Just give me a chance, Noelle. Don't run away again. Besides…your daughter is charming."

Relief washed through me followed by a flood of heat. If I hadn't been braced by his arms, I think my knees would have given out and I might have collapsed. This was not what I'd expected to hear. Hoped for, maybe, in some unguarded part of my mind and heart, but never expected. This guy may be another athlete, but what an unusual man. He seemed to speak from the heart. To hear him include Tatum soothed some of my doubts. This and spicy ice cream, too. Wow!

I looked up at his face and saw his jaw tighten and his eyes steady. This guy meant what he said. No games here. Both Tatum and the server watched us.

Zave must have noticed the server, because he let go of me and pulled out his wallet and paid the lady.

"Thank you, Tree," Tatum said, then let out a squeal of delight. "Mommy, there's Cassidy." She waved toward a little girl and her family as they entered the ice cream shop. "Can I go see her?"

Cassidy's mother, Melinda, one of my good friends, waved at me. I smiled back at her as I told Tatum to go ahead.

Zave and I walked back to the booth. We sat down across from each other. He waited while I took another taste of my ice cream, giving me a little time to put my thoughts into words.

"Look, Zave, I appreciate what you said to me. I think I have distrusted men in general for so long now that my emotions are all mixed up. I'm confused, and this…you—" I looked up at him, then continued. "— Seem like the stuff of fairy tales, kind of like a Cinderella story. I never thought I would meet a guy I would even want to date, let alone allow to meet my daughter…" My voice trailed off.

A thin stream of ice cream melted down the side of my cone. I licked it, buying time to think. I glanced over at Tatum.

She stood by her friend, laughing.

I didn't want her to hear this conversation with Zave, so I excused myself, walked over to Melinda and asked if she would keep an eye on Tatum for a few minutes.

Melinda glanced at Zave, then back at me and said, "Sure, but only if you call me tomorrow and tell me what's going on with you and that...oh, my...that's Triple X." Her mouth dropped open.

"There's not much to tell, at least not right now," I whispered. A little giggle escaped as I walked away. I was acting like a schoolgirl. I pulled myself together. It was time to come clean here with both Zave and myself.

Zave scooted over and patted the bench next to him. Needing a little space, I sat down, not quite close enough for us to touch. I angled myself so I could look at him. I took a deep breath. "Okay, I'm going to be straight with you. First of all, thank you for our ice cream. It is delicious. You're right—my former marriage was rough. I don't really want to get into it, but I will say he was not who I thought he was. I was played and bought it hook, line, and sinker.

"I left to protect my daughter and myself and because I finally realized I deserved respect. So I don't trust men, or my choices in men. Blake was a college basketball player. You're a basketball player. So yeah, this is a red flag for me. I realize I have to figure this thing out."

I paused for a moment to lick my ice cream again,

and then added in a quiet voice, "You seem like a nice guy, and yes, I'm attracted to you, but I'm a package deal now, and what is best for my little girl is at the top of my list. That's where I'm at." I looked down, avoiding his eyes.

He studied me a moment as I sat quietly eating my ice cream. I knew it was delicious, but now it seemed just cold with no flavor; even the residual spicy heat was gone. I had given him a way out. I wondered if he would take it or if he cared enough to stick around.

After what seemed like an eternity, he broke the silence.

"Noelle, I'm not sure what is going on here with us, but I do know this. There is something rare about you and Tatum, and I can't quit thinking about you both. Each time I see you, I feel the same way. I don't want to just run into you by chance anymore. I would like to stick around and get to know you, and I hope that as you get to know me, you will see that I'm not like Blake, or any other guy, for that matter." He paused then added, "What do you think? May I see you two again?"

I didn't hesitate with my answer. I had spoken my heart, and he had respected what I said. "Yes. As long as you continue to always be straight with me. And I will always be honest with you, too." I smiled at him. A feeling of peace settled over me for the first time in a long time.

"Agreed." He beamed.

I licked a spot of ice cream off my lip.

Zave focused on my mouth. His eyes changed to a deep jade green, and he leaned toward me. Heart racing, I closed my eyes, thinking he was going to kiss my lips.

Instead, I felt a soft kiss on my forehead.

Surprised, I opened my eyes in time to see that big lopsided grin. Then his face softened once again. I saw longing, hope, desire, as he brought his head down again and this time—

"Hey, check it out, guys. It's Triple X, and he's about to lay one on that Frost reporter lady." A bunch of whooping and hollering followed.

Zave and I jumped apart and turned toward the noise. A group of tall, lanky teens wearing various pieces of basketball attire had entered the ice cream store.

"Yeah, and she is not 'frosty'…she's downright hot," added one of the teens, and they burst out laughing again.

"I better go talk to those guys so they'll leave us alone—especially you, hot Frost lady." He gave my hand a quick squeeze, then headed over to the high schoolers.

****

Zave followed our car back to my condo and walked us to the front door.

The setting sun over the dark purple mountains to the west blazed its last few streaks of light for the evening before succumbing to dusk. The autumn air smelled sweet, and leaves crunched under our feet.

Tatum grabbed Zave's hand to get his attention. "Can you come to my school tomorrow? I want to show everyone that I know a giant. I told Hunter, but he doesn't believe me."

Zave didn't miss a beat. "Yes, I'll come to your school, but how about if I talk to your teacher and principal first to make sure it's okay if a giant comes to

45

visit?"

"Oh, yeah. Maybe you better. They might call the sheriffissess, 'cause there's a giant at the school." She smiled her sweetest smile at him.

"Tell Zave thanks for the ice cream, then head in, and get your jammies on, sweetie. I'll be there in a few minutes."

"Thank you, Tree." She threw her arms around one of his long legs, hugged it, and skipped into the condo and up the stairs singing, "Tree is coming to school. Tree is coming to school."

Zave stood there looking dumbfounded, his head cocked to one side, staring where Tatum had disappeared inside the house. After a moment, he glanced down at me and said, "She knows how to wiggle right into your heart, doesn't she?"

"Yes, she is wonderful. I'm super lucky." Warmth flooded me. I realized then that this giant of a man was nothing more than a big softy.

Zave reached out and took my hand. I raised our hands up and explored his in the porch light as he silently observed. Most of his palm and fingers were rough, as I would expect a farmer's or rancher's hands to be. He must have earned all these callouses from handling basketballs. I enjoyed the warmth and strength in his large hand. I felt safe and secure.

He adjusted his hand so our fingers intertwined.

It felt comfortable. It seemed right. I looked up at him again to see a slight smile on his face.

He seemed to feel it, too.

He took my other hand and with a boyish grin said, "Game next Friday night?"

"Uhh, you have a game next Friday?" I looked at

him, confused.

"Yes. It's pre-season, but I meant to say, would you like to come to the game Friday night?"

"This Friday?" I asked.

"No, we have a few games out of town this weekend, so it would be the next Friday." His face had a look of a hopeful little boy. This man kept getting more adorable. He had a reputation for being a tough guy on the court, but he sure had a tender side. What a dichotomy.

"Sure." I almost laughed.

His shoulders dropped in relief, as if he had been holding his breath.

"I'll send a car for you. I'd like to take you to my favorite restaurant for dinner after."

I stuck both hands in my pockets. I felt myself pull back a bit. It was all too new. "Rolling out the red carpet, are you?"

His slow grin grew into a full-out sensory charge. I could get used to that smile. Then my stomach hosted another butterfly race, and I wondered what it would be like to touch that smile, to run my finger over the outline, then...

"Mommy, are you coming?" interrupted my daydream.

Both of us jolted.

It seemed he was having his own little daydream.

This could be fun, or this could be trouble.

"Slow down, Elle." I realized I'd said that out loud and followed it with a "No!" I fumbled over my explanation. "I didn't mean to say 'slow down' out loud and then tell myself 'no.' I was trying to tell myself to slow down, then not to say it out loud. Oh, never mind…" I faded off, too embarrassed.

Zave let out a hearty laugh. "Noelle Frost, you are full of surprises. I don't think things will ever be dull with you." He chuckled. "I'll take off now. Tell Miss Tatum thanks for spending some time with me this evening. I'll call you tomorrow so we can make plans for next Friday." He took a step closer and reached up with the tip of a finger and traced my lips.

My lips came alive and pulsed with the beat of my heart. Zave's soft, slow touch lingered long after he was gone.

Chapter Nine

I stepped into the Mason Jar and took a deep breath to enjoy the comforting smell of fried chicken and freshly baked bread as it wafted around the cozy restaurant. I spotted my three sisters in our favorite wooden booth with a cheery red and white gingham tablecloth. Taking a deep breath, I squared my shoulders and joined them, expecting a major grilling concerning my love life, thanks to my phone conversation with Chrissy the week before.

We greeted each other with the customary warm hugs on our Friday night sisters dinner out. Then sure enough, the moment we placed our orders, the inquisition began.

"Spill it, sister." Joy's face lit up.

"Yeah, do tell, Elle," added Chrissy, snickering.

"Give us the scoop," chimed in Holly with a huge grin.

I groaned at her jibe at me being a reporter, then took a moment to compose myself as I sipped ice water with a slice of fresh lime. "I'm sure Chrissy already filled you in, and there's not much more to tell."

"Oh, come on, you have to give us more than that," Joy demanded.

"Well, ummm…his name is Zave. He's really tall and gorgeous." I couldn't stop my huge grin.

All three sisters stared at me for a moment.

"That's it? That's all you're going to share?" Holly's shoulders slumped.

"Okay, okay. Tatum and I did have ice cream with him the other night, and he isn't what I expected."

"How so?" asked Chrissy.

"You know when you're talking to someone and they are super interested in everything you say, not faking it to be courteous, but kind of looking into your soul?" I paused, realizing I had shared some deep stuff instead of keeping it light. Oh well, it was too late now, plus my sisters were my best friends and I was safe with them.

No one answered. All three looked at me with wide eyes.

Finally, Joy cleared her throat and leaned toward me, her voice clear and lower than usual. "Elle, Chrissy shared with us who this guy is, and well…" She faded off and glanced at Holly and Chrissy, who both nodded to tell her to continue.

"He's the biggest player there is, and he's in the news a lot—often connected to gorgeous, famous women." Joy flattened her hands on the table.

"Why tell you three busybodies anything? I knew you wouldn't approve of me seeing another basketball player, but I had hoped you would be happy that I'm at least showing a little interest in a man." My mouth tightened.

"Well, we're concerned, that's for sure," Holly said, leaning toward me.

"Yeah, Elle. We don't want to see you hurt again." Chrissy furrowed her brows.

I took a deep breath and raised my chin. "Look, I know there's a number of loser athletes in my past, but maybe, just maybe, I can break that horrible chain. Good guys and bad guys come in all shapes and sizes—and have a variety of careers."

"Sure, but you tend to go for the really tall ones," Chrissy giggled.

"Okay, you're right, but please hear me out, dear sisters of mine. I'm scared—very scared. I mean, after that horrible Blake mess, I decided I was done. And I mean really done. The only decent men on this earth were Dad and your husband, Joy—and they're both gone." I paused and dropped my head. I missed them both so much.

The noise of silverware clanking and voices talking filled the air as we sisters sat deep in thought.

"Here, let me refill your waters," our waitress said, interrupting our sad memories.

"So with my distrust in men, I had decided all men were jerks, and Tatum and I were better off without them." I took another sip of my water. My stomach churned. Facing my sisters was as tough as I thought it would be.

"So what about Triple X? What makes him different?" Holly asked.

"First, let me explain what it's taken me the past four and a half years and a divorce to figure out." I looked directly at Holly, then added, "A relationship doesn't have anything to do with a sport; it has to do with the man. The key is vanity and narcissism. Some men think the world revolves around them, like a two-year-old who won't grow up."

Holly nodded.

Encouraged, I continued, "Then when they excel at something, especially sports, people tend to give them a free ride. Everyone adores them, kisses up to them, and pretty soon they believe all the hype. I think it goes so far that in some situations they begin to objectify others, especially women. Everyone is there for their will or pleasure."

I paused again, thinking about my ex-husband. "And then…if they have a temper—a nasty temper—well, that's something I won't ever go near again."

I had never voiced any of this to them before. I glanced around at everyone. Each watched me with eyes squinted as if they were pondering what I'd said. I hoped they would understand.

"Sounds like your ex, for sure," said Chrissy, and the other two nodded in agreement. "You definitely know what to avoid in a man."

"Elle, you know we've all been worried about you, but what you're telling us makes sense. It sounds like you're ready to move forward and real healing is beginning to happen." Joy's eyes watered as she gave me a sweet and gentle smile, much like our mother had always done when we had heart-to-heart talks.

My stomach relaxed. I leaned closer to the table. "I'm determined not to make that same mistake again. I'm going into this with my eyes wide open, and believe me, I'm well aware of the risks, especially with Tatum as part of the equation. I owe it to both of us to follow my brains this time and not just my heart. I'm getting to know Zave, and so far, he's real. He's been open and honest and doesn't seem to be the player the press makes him out to be."

We all smiled because I was part of that press, although they knew I would never write gossip.

"Plus, I promise each of you that I will move

slowly." I looked directly into each of their eyes.

"But what do you really know about this guy?" Holly asked.

"Well, he's kind and service oriented—not big headed. Basketball is just his job. He's worked hard to be where he is. He runs a youth basketball camp in the summer. He takes time with fans…and their mothers." I couldn't help smiling as I thought of the interaction between the mother asking Zave for an autograph for her son when we were at the ice cream parlor, then continued. "He's a downright normal guy. He seems to stay in close contact with his parents and siblings." I knew I was rambling, but once the flood gates opened, I had to let it all out.

"And yes, I'm a little worried about all the photos with different girls on his arm at various events. I'm trying to go into this with my eyes open. It may take some time to figure out for sure and…of course, if he isn't an honest, kind, loyal man with a good temper, then I'm out." My stomach tightened.

"How do you know all this stuff about him already?" Chrissy asked.

"Well, umm…" These were my sisters and I really needed them to understand that I was looking at all angles. "Maybe I played reporter and uh…did some research, and since he's famous, he has a pretty good media trail."

They laughed.

"Oh, come on. Open eyes, remember? Plus, I promised myself not to be bowled over by his good looks and those tantalizing green eyes." I sighed and faded off into another memory.

All three grinned at me.

"I know, I know, I sound like a stalker. But there could be a lot at stake here and I needed to check out things from all sides. I'm not going to make the same mistake I made falling for Blake."

All my sisters sat quietly for a few moments. Finally, Joy said, "You know, Elle, I don't think what you did was stalking. Just like any story you write; you want to know the truth. I think checking him out is a good idea."

Holly and Chrissy nodded in agreement, then Chrissy added, "I say good for you, girl. You have an unusual situation here, and you have to play it safe."

"Yes, and you're going into this thing logically, if love even has logic. Give it a chance, Elle," Holly agreed.

I sat back in relief. My sisters seemed to be getting what I was going through.

"This is exciting, for sure…but it also feels like I'm in a bit of a whirlwind. I don't want to be hurt again, and I certainly don't want Tatum hurt." I took another sip before I went on. "Tatum adores him already. She told him he could marry me, but that's a whole other story."

"She what?" Joy demanded.

"Tell all, Elle," Chrissy added, eyes wide.

"This is going to be good." Holly licked her lips.

I gave in. "All right, long story short. Tatum says she and her little school friend, Hunter, are getting married when they're eight. Hunter and his dad watched one of my news stories and both decided they might marry me. Hunter mentioned it to Tatum, Tatum was crushed, so asked me to marry Hunter's dad or 'the Tree'—her name for Zave—then Hunter could still marry her." I took a quick breath, and then went on.

"I told her not to worry because I wasn't planning on ever getting married again. She was thrilled, and now she and Hunter are still on for their big childhood wedding. When we had ice cream with Zave Wednesday, Tatum blurted all this out to him. Here's the sticky part. She added that he could marry me because she'd like that."

The sisters whooped and hollered.

"No!" Joy slapped her knee. "That's horrible...and hilarious."

I laughed with them.

When the laughter died down, Holly asked, "So what did the poor guy do?"

"Zave took it all quite well and wants us to be in the picture. He's different from any other man I've met. He's a nice man and sincerely seems to want to get to know me, plus his interaction with Tatum is charming. He's considerate of his fans, has incredible green eyes, has a great job he enjoys, is hard-working, fun, and fun to look at..." I trailed off as a trio of groans greeted me, almost in three-part harmony.

"Okay, you guys, please give me a break. I feel I want to give this a chance, so please support me. Don't make this harder than it already is. I mean, I have enough lack of trust in the male species for all four of us."

The waitress saved the day as she placed our dinners on the table.

"Oh, my. Smell these baby-back ribs." I took a big, mouth-watering sniff. "Joy, your pot pie crust looks perfect. Holly, did you get that goulashy thing again? It does look delicious. Chrissy, how about a few onion rings?"

Each of them smirked at me, knowing exactly what I was doing, but the comfort food here was to die for, so we all dug in and enjoyed it.

I tried to listen to their conversation, but soon those intense green eyes made their way back to my thoughts, and I sat anticipating Zave's upcoming late-night phone call. He'd been calling me most nights while on his road trip.

I tuned back to the concerns my sisters had and caution hit. Fear zapped the rest of my appetite. Zave's press showed he had women around him constantly. He led a life in the spotlight.

I didn't know him well enough to know if he was a faithful, one-woman kind of a guy—someone with high integrity around women. Plus, in the back of my mind I still worried there might be something wrong with me that made me choose abusive men who tended to cheat.

With Blake, I allowed myself to believe the abuse was my fault. But now I knew better. The abuse was his responsibility. I didn't have to listen to his excuses or believe his lies anymore. I was stronger now.

I didn't want to shut out Zave because of fear. I needed to get to know him better so I could make a clear judgment with more than my heart and those traitor butterflies making the decisions. Those phone calls had helped because we had conversation without the physical side getting in the way.

I planned to move slow, keep my heart safe, get to know the real man, and not fall for another narcissistic, womanizing jerk.

There, that would work just fine…a good plan.

Besides, it had been a long time since I kissed a

man…and since I was being totally honest about all of this, I really looked forward to our first kiss.

Chapter Ten

"Mommy, get up." Tatum pounced on my bed.

I didn't know what time it was, but any time I was awakened from a deep sleep was too early. I reached out and wrapped my arms around the little monkey and pulled her under the covers. "Snuggle in and go back to sleep."

"Mah-ah-ahm! Wake up. Tree can see through the TV." She put her face so close our noses touched.

"Wha-a-a-t?" I yawned and stretched.

"He said 'Hi' and told me to go to bed. Oh, and he said I'm the cutest thing on the planet, too."

"What? Honey, you're not making any sense. Tree had a game in Phoenix last night. And what do you mean, he talked to you?" I gently pushed her away so I wouldn't go crossed-eyed.

"He did, last night while you were gone. I was in bed, but my tummy growled and wanted a cupcake, so I snucked into the kitchen. The babysitter had basketball on, and didn't see me 'cause I'm tricky, but Tree is trickier, 'cause he saw me through the TV. This reporter lady said stuff, and then he looked at me through the TV. Get up, Mamma."

I sat up and ran my fingers through my hair, scratching my head. How strange. Tatum made no sense.

"Come on. I'll show you." She tugged at my hand.

I let out a big sigh. Sleeping in...not on the agenda after all. I trudged down the stairs to the family room.

Tatum turned on the TV and handed me the remote. "Go fast to the end. Tree is magic."

I found the recorded game and fast forwarded to the end. Shoot, now I knew they won. I had planned on watching the game last night, but the gas explosion I covered had run late into the night. Oh well, I'd still watch it later. I didn't want to miss any of Zave's games—or Zave. I paused, then forwarded slowly through a bunch of commercials until I saw his large and quite fine frame next to a sandy-haired reporter.

"Yeah, here." Tatum bounced on the sofa next to me.

The reporter held the microphone up to her mouth and spoke loudly over the still cheering crowd. "Another triple tonight, Triple X. I did a little fact checking and found that you have passed Wilt Chamberlain and Russel Westbrook's records of thirty-one triple doubles. You're closing in on Oscar Robinson's forty-one triple doubles from 1962. Is this what your legacy will be?"

Zave leaned down to the microphone and answered, "I just try to play my best each game."

"Throughout your career you've had a number of nicknames. The Green-Eyed Giant in high school, Thunder Mountain in college, and now of course, Triple X. Which is your favorite?" The reporter flashed a big smile and giggled as if she had said something clever. A little green-eyed monster reared up in me. She sure knew a lot about Zave, and she was totally trying to flirt.

"My favorite nickname? I think that would be

Tree." Zave smiled his big, lopsided grin and looked directly into the camera, then added, "Hi, Tatum. Get to bed—it's late."

"Hold on. We hear rumors of Rhonda Santori, the team owner's daughter…Uh…who's Tatum?"

Zave laughed. "Never believe rumors. I can tell you this, though. Tatum is about the cutest thing on the planet." He winked into the camera, turned, and walked toward the locker room.

Apparently, the interview was over.

The reporter seemed surprised but pulled herself together quickly. "Well, umm…more on this soon, I'm sure." She tossed it back to the sportscasters.

"Well, okay then." I fell back against the sofa, chuckling.

"See, Mommy? Tree can see me. Isn't that soooo cool? Can I have a cupcake for breakfast?"

"How about if I whip up a banana smoothie with that cupcake?" I followed her to the kitchen, amazed at the simple brilliance and wonder of children, especially my adorable little girl…and Zave wasn't half bad himself. I smiled.

Chapter Eleven

The weather turned frosty on Friday, a week before my big date. Little shivers of excitement raced around my skin each time I thought about it, and I had to keep telling myself to calm down and not read too much into it. It was only a date, and I certainly wasn't ready for it to be anything more. Besides, I had to play it cool. I was meeting my sisters at the Mason Jar again.

I dropped Tatum off at her friend's house for the evening. She gave me a quick hug and ran inside.

"Thanks for watching her, Melinda."

"My pleasure. We thought we would watch one of their favorite princess movies after we eat pizza."

"Sounds great. I won't be late."

"No worries. I still expect an update about you and Triple X soon." Melinda smiled.

My mouth fell open. I stammered, "Uh well, there really isn't much to say...yet. This is...ummm well, all so new."

"He's a looker. Fingers crossed, girlfriend. Have fun with your sisters," she said and gave me a hug.

The drive to the Mason Jar took me a few minutes. I parked, walked into the restaurant, and found Holly and Chrissy sitting in our usual booth. Once again, the smells of fried chicken and warm bread made my mouth water. This place always brought up the sweet memories of being a little girl in my mother's kitchen.

I squared my shoulders, preparing myself to act as if nothing new had been going on in the romance department. Joy walked in a minute or so after me, and behind her came a familiar face from the past.

Joy blurted out, "Look who showed up at my house a few minutes ago."

Uncle Simon, Dad's older brother, strode across the restaurant toward us with a movie star smile.

My stomach lurched. My nerves moved to high alert and my guard came up. Uncle Simon wasn't around much when we were kids. If I asked Dad about him, Dad always brushed the question off by saying something like, "Simon has gone his own way. It's for the best." There seemed to be a sadness or sorrow in Dad when I brought Uncle Simon up. I learned not to mention him.

Chrissy shrieked, "Oh, you look just like Dad." She jumped up, and he pulled her into a big bear hug.

Next, he pulled me up out of my seat and wrapped me in his arms. I offered him a quiet "Hello" as I silently questioned Joy with my eyes.

Uncomfortable, I pulled away. This man was mostly a stranger to me. Uncle Simon gave Holly a hug, and I saw her hesitation as well. My reporter skills or maybe my sixth sense kicked in. All I could think of was why wasn't he here when our parents died four years ago? And why was he here now?

He pulled a chair up to the end of the booth and sat down. "You're all so lovely. What have each of you been doing? I met Joy's three rambunctious boys. How about you, Elle?" Simon folded his arms across his chest and sat back against his chair.

My hands clamped closed in my lap as I gave a

short answer. "I'm a reporter for CBS 4 Denver, divorced, and have a five-year-old daughter."

Simon nodded his head with a slight smile that didn't reach his eyes, and then turned his attention to Holly. "And what are you doing now?"

"I'm a nurse, like Mom, you know. I work at the local hospital," Holly answered.

"I knew you would do well, Holly." Simon's face lit up in a large grin. "And what about you, little lady? What have you been up to?" He turned to Chrissy.

"I've graduated college and have a great job in marketing. I love it," Chrissy gushed.

I watched this weird scene unfold in front of me with an uneasy feeling growing in my stomach. I guess my sisters were more comfortable than me with the re-appearance of long-lost Uncle Simon. Especially Joy and Chrissy.

The waitress arrived. None of us was ready to order. Simon's appearance had us all enthralled, each with our own reasons.

Simon turned his attention back to us. "I am so happy to be back in the Springs," he said.

"Have you moved back, then?" I asked.

"Yes, I bought a condo, and I'm furnishing it now."

"That's wonderful. We hope to see a lot of you," Chrissy beamed.

I remained silent, assessing the situation, my reporter skills tingling. After an awkward pause, I asked, "What business are you in, Simon? Or are you retired now?"

He chuckled. "Oh no. I'm a consultant. Keeps me busy traveling all over the world. It's an exciting profession with a new challenge always waiting around the corner." He cleared his throat, seeming a little nervous, and then sipped his water. "I've worked with scores of big businesses—and a number of small ones, too. I like to help others, especially when it comes to money."

When he seemed finished, I blurted out, "Oh? Well, Uncle Simon, it's been extremely…difficult, especially losing Mom and Dad, and Joy's husband, Tom. Where have you been all this time?"

He dropped his eyes and his shoulders slumped. "I've been in Europe. I didn't know about your parents until many months later, or I would have been here to help. Then…time moved on, and before I knew it, several years had passed."

I knew I had been rude. I offered a small token of peace. "I hope things go well for you here. Welcome back."

Uncle Simon smiled and chatted a few more minutes, then he asked to see us again. He and Joy exchanged phone numbers before he left.

We sat quietly, lost in our own thoughts. I still felt a little agitated but wasn't exactly sure why. Again, Dad came to mind. He had seemed content that Uncle Simon was not a part of our lives. I also realized that even though my faith in my own judgment took a big hit from my time with Blake, I needed to learn to listen to my gut. And until I knew what was behind the sudden reappearance of Uncle Simon, I would remain a little leery.

In fact, I wasn't ready to think of him as "Uncle." That was an endearment that he needed to earn. So he was just Simon to me for now.

We picked at our food. Chrissy seemed nearly overwhelmed with the possibility of having an uncle in our lives, and Joy and Holly remarked on his good looks and high-end clothes and watch. He must be rich, we all agreed. What a mystery.

I decided to use my reporting skills to do a little investigating on my own. One good thing about his surprise appearance was at least I didn't have to try to avoid questions from my sisters about Zave.

Chapter Twelve

I had been anticipating Friday for two weeks now. Even though it was preseason, it was my first Denver Nuggets game as the guest of a player. Sure, I'd been with friends, even taken Tatum to a few games, but never as a VIP. And not just any player—Triple X. I mean, wow! When I thought of him that way, I was in awe. The guy I knew was more comfortable going by the name "Tree" and was kind, funny, caring, adorable, hot, and…well, so much more than the nation's most eligible big-shot basketball player.

Holly had called earlier in the week asking for some play time with her favorite—and only—niece, so Tatum was spending the night with her, and I didn't need to worry how late I stayed out.

I took a shower and spent way too long on my hair and makeup. Earlier in the week I'd purchased a new pair of jeans, shoes, and a sky-blue peplum blouse with a cute little soft, ruffled strip at the bottom. I topped it all off with a chunky, gold bling necklace to match the team colors. Spending so much time prepping reminded me of the fun times getting ready for high school proms.

I packed an overnight bag. One of the CBS 4 station's perks available to employees was a condo in Denver. I had booked it for tonight so I wouldn't have to make the hour drive after the game and late dinner.

I called Holly and asked to talk to Tatum.

"Hi, sweetie. School go okay today?"

"Yeah, Mommy. Me and Cassidy chased the boys up the big tree. They got in trouble."

I stifled a laugh. "You mean 'Cassidy and I' chased the boys up the big tree."

"Nooooo, Mommy. Me and Cassidy chased the boys, not you. You weren't there." She sounded perturbed.

"Okay. Silly me. We'll have this grammar discussion another time. What are you and Aunt Holly doing tonight?"

"We're going to eat pizza with pepper-no-knees." Her voice rose with excitement.

I grinned. Tatum often said words phonetically, the way she heard them. "Yes, I'm sure you will. Now don't stay up too late. I love you, Tatum."

"I love you too, Mommy. Bye."

I slipped my phone into my purse. The doorbell rang.

"Ms. Frost? Your carriage awaits." A young man in what I took to be a Denver-Nugget-blue suit saluted me, then walked to the sleek, black stretch limo and opened the door. "There's a fridge in the center with sodas, bottled water, and snacks. If you need anything, I'm the fourth button down."

A glass wall rose directly behind his seat, and I was all alone in this new world. I giggled. I was Cinderella. Delighted, I rummaged around the mini-fridge and chose water and an apple, and then sat in the back row. One of the buttons built into the wall said "Roof." I pushed it. Half of the ceiling opened up to the lovely, clear sky. A few early evening stars winked at me as the crisp, autumn air heightened my senses.

Another button said "Recline." I pushed it and my chair did just that, with a footrest and all. I leaned back with a sigh of sheer pleasure.

I watched people drive by, rubbernecking to see who was inside the limo. This must be what animals in the zoo felt like, except the windows were tinted so they couldn't see inside. What a first date. This was already too much fun. The anticipation of a wonderful evening continued to build.

The limo stopped near the elevator under the Pepsi Center. I thanked the chauffeur and was greeted by a young lady who handed me a lanyard with a VIP/Nuggets pass. What a thrill. No parking problems. No long walk to the stadium. No hassle. I could get used to this.

Then that little devil of doubt on my shoulder had to interject, "How many other women have received this kind of treatment by Zave?"

I shook my head to clear it. What he did before he met me was really none of my business. On the other hand, I might ask him anyway, so I could begin to build some trust. "Eyes wide open, Elle." I spoke out loud. In the meantime, I chose to enjoy the pampering.

The elevator opened into a large hallway leading to the basketball court. The young lady showed me to my seat, announced that food and drink were on the house, and then left.

Front row, ground floor, near the center of the basketball court—it didn't get any better than that.

People ambled around, finding their seats. A husband and wife sat next to me and introduced themselves. They were long-time fans and major financial contributors to the team. A little old lady with blue hair sat on my other side—not old-lady-blue hair, Denver-Nugget-blue. She was a riot. She told me she lived for the games. I believed her.

The lights dimmed and the noisy crowd hushed as the disco ball attached to the jumbotron spun, bouncing light everywhere. Music blared, and as it reached a crescendo, the Denver Nuggets, led by Triple X, jogged onto the floor. It was strange to see him out there with all those other big guys, and I mean big. Up close they looked like a forest of giants. They stood in a line, and as "The Star-Spangled Banner" played, I watched Zave, with his hand over his heart, search the crowd—until he saw me.

A huge smile split his face, and he did that head-nod thing that guys do. I grinned back. A tingle buzzed through my body.

Zave made eye contact and beamed at me after each basket he made, and oh, that smile. I cheered as loud as the blue-haired lady next to me, hoping to see that smile again.

During halftime, I stepped into the restroom and ran into Rhonda, the team owner's daughter, dressed in painted-on white pants and Nugget-blue halter top. She did a double take, as if she recognized me, but didn't say anything.

I thought, she certainly wasn't afraid to show a little skin, and those stiletto heels—if I wore those, I'd break my ankles.

As she gobbed sticky lipstick on unnaturally puffy lips and admired herself in the mirror, she talked to her friend, who was dressed in similar attire.

I heard Zave's name and scooted closer to listen.

"Triple X is looking hot tonight. Did you see him smiling at me every time he made a basket? The guy has it bad for me." Rhonda fluffed her hair.

"You have it bad for Triple X, you mean." The other girl leaned into the mirror and applied some mascara on her already heavily coated fake lashes.

I didn't care to hear any more. I tossed my paper towel into the trash and left. The lady who helped me to my seat appeared by my side and asked if she could get me anything to eat or drink.

"A half blue-raspberry, half-cherry snow cone, please."

She gave me an odd look.

"A little strange, I know—a favorite from my childhood, kind of comfort food." And I needed some comfort food right now. Seeing and hearing Rhonda had upset me more than I thought. Zave may not be into her, but she had her hooks out for him.

"Calm down, Elle," I muttered in an effort to reassure myself. "Remember, Zave invited you. He already told you he wants nothing to do with her. Focus on that. There will always be Rhondas out there. This is part of learning to trust again." My mumbled self-talk worked as I made my way back to my seat.

I enjoyed watching several people attempt to make shots from the half-court line to win cars. No one did, but the crowd hooted and hollered anyway. Glancing around, I noticed Rhonda and her little friend a few rows behind me. No wonder she thought those smiles were for her.

My snow cone arrived as the teams jogged in to warm up. I leaned back in my chair and enjoyed my treat. I was a kid on a hot summer day nibbling on my favorite snack and watching my favorite show. I received more smiles from Zave, sending shivers to my toes.

The little old blue-haired lady tapped me on the shoulder. "I noticed that handsome Xavier smiling this way each time he makes a shot. Is he, by chance, smiling at you?"

"I sure hope so. He's pretty cute, isn't he?" I grinned.

"Oh yes, my dear, and if I were a few decades younger, I would make a play for him." She gave me a cheeky grin. "I'm Verlayne, by the way, Verlayne Sample. Hey, I know you. You're Noelle Frost, the TV reporter."

"Guilty as charged." I flashed my TV smile at her.

"You two will have some beautiful children." She gave me a calculating look.

My face was as hot as a sunburn. "Uh, we're just friends."

"That's good. Always be friends. That makes for a good marriage. He's a nice boy, and I like you." She reached up and gave me a big hug. Her blue hair smelled like peroxide and a good dose of what reminded me of a vintage perfume called Windsong.

The crowd roared, and we focused on the rest of the game. Another win for the Nuggets. The team ambled down the tunnel to the locker room, but Zave and a few other players stuck around to do TV and radio interviews.

Then Zave, towel around his neck, walked over to where I sat and held out his hand. I placed my hand in his and couldn't help noticing, again, how huge it was. I loved how safe it made me feel.

"Come with me, lovely lady." He squeezed my hand. "So…did you enjoy the game?"

"Loved it." I squeezed his hand back. "You were amazing!"

"It was amazing to have you here in the stands." Another one of his lopsided grins appeared.

My heart pounded. "I loved the smiles per basket. You must have made a million tonight." I looked up at him. He was flushed, sweat covered, and gorgeous.

"We'll have to see if we can exchange baskets for kisses. What do you think?"

I tingled all over and laughed. "Umm, we'll see," and then thought, snappy answer, Elle. What I wanted to say was, "Not a bad idea. I'm looking forward to our first kiss, big guy."

We walked through the tunnel, and near the end Zave opened a large glass door and said, "Please wait here for me while I get showered and changed, okay?"

"Sure." I walked across the spacious room and plopped into a large, cushy chair near the wall. I had some time to think. I second-guessed developing a relationship with another athlete. So far, there was nothing in his character that gave me any doubts about him. I needed to get to the point where I trusted again. Not just normal trust, either. His life in the spotlight was not normal. I knew I was totally jumping the gun, but it was fun to be silly and dream of a possible future together.

Both of us would travel at times, me with stories, Zave with road trips. He was a superstar in the world of basketball and would always be treated differently. If I attached my star to his wagon, I would be judged by his world, too. That was okay. I didn't have anything to hide. Sure, this may not work out, but if it did, I needed to decide if I could handle what it would take to be with a superstar.

I thought of Tatum. Zave was adorable with her, and she thought "Tree" was great, so no worries there. How would his fame affect her? Well, we would keep things as normal as possible for her…and any new little ones, that's for sure. My musings stopped short when Rhonda and her friend entered, giggling.

"He got to me with all those smiles tonight. I'm sure he'll take me out to dinner." She plopped on a seat near the door. "Want to get one of the other players and go with us?

"Like who?" asked mini-Rhonda.

"I don't know. Pick another player. They're all hot." Rhonda slouched in the chair and stretched her long legs out in front of her.

"The Streak—he makes my blood boil." Mini-Rhonda shook her shoulders as if a shiver had run through her body.

"Okay. Here they come. Let's go out there and do some serious flirting." Rhonda and friend headed out the door toward a group of players coming from the locker room.

How ridiculous. I shook my head, glad the two of them hadn't noticed me. I walked to the door to watch for Zave and saw him walking behind several guys.

Rhonda stepped around them and tucked her arm through Zave's. He stopped and carefully removed it. She shoved it back. He peeled it away again and took a big step back, creating distance between them. He spoke to her for a moment and then continued walking.

She stood in place, shoulders drooping. A second

or two later, she thrust her chin up and caught up to him once more. This time she stepped in front of him and wrapped her arms around his neck.

Zave tilted his head back, away from her, then gently, but firmly pushed her off and pinned her arms down by her sides. He held her there as he spoke. When he let go, she stomped her foot—actually stomped it, like a toddler throwing a tantrum. Zave kept walking.

Okay then, he was a man of his word. Rhonda was not in the picture. I felt a smile forming as I stepped out of the lounge and joined him. We walked hand in hand down the hall. I chanced a glance at Rhonda.

Her mouth dropped open, and her eyes shot lasers at me.

Ignoring her, we caught the elevator to the team parking area. Zave held the door of his black Jeep Renegade open for me, then hopped in the driver's side. I saw the elevator open again and Rhonda exited. She watched us as we drove out of the parking lot. Though she was spoiled and scheming, she seemed the epitome of the "poor little rich girl."

Chapter Thirteen

Once we left the parking area, I relaxed. "Where're we going?"

"Dinner." Zave took my hand again. I liked the way our hands fit together. I felt the hard calluses. No pansy, soft mitts on this guy. A sense of security filled me. No one's going to pick a fight with a six-foot ten inch giant.

"Zave, I have a question for you."

"Shoot." He grinned.

"Nice pun, basketball man. Why is your jersey number thirteen? Most people consider it unlucky."

"I first set eyes on you on August thirteenth. That was one of my luckiest days, for sure." He tightened his hold on my hand and butterflies did the cha-cha in my stomach.

"Hold it. You've been number thirteen for years. Seriously, why thirteen?"

"Since I was a little kid, good things happened to me on the thirteenth—especially on Fridays that are the thirteenths. It might be a known bad luck day for others, but for me, the thirteenth has always been lucky. Meeting you on the thirteenth really was lucky." He glanced at me, then flashed that adorable lop-sided grin.

Oh, be still my heart. "You're quite the sweet-talker, aren't you?" I asked, and not wholly in jest. I mean, with all the women flaunting themselves at him, why was he still available?

"Nah, actually, I usually get kind of tongue-tied around the fairer sex in one-on-one situations."

"No way."

"Way. You ladies tie me up in knots. Give me a basketball and a bunch of tough guys to battle in a gym, no problem, but girls making plays? No, thank you."

"Is that how it always was?" My eyebrows raised in surprise.

"Yeah, pretty much since high school. People see me as a commodity, an object. Most want something from me, and the ladies aren't any different. I don't want adoration. I definitely don't want one-night stands. I don't want to be wanted for my money or fame. I don't want to date girls who chase me because I'm Triple X. I'm tired of calculating females."

"What do you want?"

"I want someone who sees me for me, just Xavier Maximillian Trayce, or Zave, or Tree." He gave me a sideways glance with the corners of his mouth raised, and then continued, "I'm a normal guy who happens to play basketball for a living. I want the chance to have a real life out of the spotlight."

Zave paused for a moment as if to gather his thoughts, or maybe his courage, and then he lowered his voice to an almost whisper. "I want to have a wife who knows the real me and loves me in spite of all my faults. I want a family, a big family. I want the whole thing—dirty diapers and all—you know, runny noses, kids waking me up by pouncing on me. I want to be happy, like my parents."

Wow, he was so different from my ex-husband. All Blake wanted was the opposite of what Zave expressed.

"You ready to run now? That was a lot to dump on you, and I usually don't talk about that stuff." He seemed a little nervous and remained silent as I sat quietly thinking for a few minutes.

I liked what he said. He wasn't anything like his public reputation. "You know, not many guys own up to what you said, and it's refreshing. I don't like games and hidden agendas. It seems like we are looking for a lot of the same things in life. I have a head start on my family with Tatum, and she means the world to me."

I glanced over at him.

He glanced back and gave me a soft grin, then focused back on the road.

I continued, "I appreciate you sharing what you said with me because it helps me know you as Zave, not Triple X. I have a silly question for you, though. Do you want a little house with a white picket fence?" I stifled a little giggle.

He laughed, and then said, "I would settle for a roomy house with a number of acres for the family to run and play on." Then he smirked as he said, "I'm not the glossy, socialite guy the press seems to like to flaunt. Do I have warts and character flaws? Yup, hundreds."

We laughed together.

"You know, Noelle, you're easy to talk to—guess that's why you're such a good TV reporter—that and you're sure easy to look at." A sexy dimple flashed on his cheek and then his face turned serious. "I feel like I'm just Zave, and you're Noelle. No hype here. Thank you." He gave my hand another squeeze.

His sincerity touched my heart. Before I had a chance to comment, he made a turn and parked the

Jeep. He bounded out and opened my door for me.

"Brownie points for being a gentleman."

"Did you say, 'brownie points for being a gentleman'?" Zave asked with a chuckle.

"Uh…I guess I did. Sorry, my talking out loud gets me in trouble sometimes." I squirmed.

He grinned and said, "But just the same, I'm glad I earned some brownie points. Do they add to the number of kisses exchanged for baskets?"

"Wait a minute. I didn't agree to exchange kisses for baskets." I noticed we were walking up some stairs and had come to a door with a dark window.

"Why? Don't you want to kiss me?"

"You're a little sure of yourself, aren't you?" I elbowed him in the ribs.

He let out an "Oomph" and then said, "Foul."

"No ref, no foul, big guy."

He laughed again.

"What is this place?" We stood at the top of the stairs on a small landing with a sign that said "Deliveries between 6:00—8:00 AM only."

Zave ignored my question as he pulled out a key and opened the door. "I'm onto you. You did your reporter thing, avoiding answering my question by asking a question of your own. It's not going to work."

He took my offending elbow and guided me down the hall into an empty restaurant. The only source of light was a crystal candelabra blazing in the middle of a table by a gigantic wall of glass overlooking the city lights of Denver. The view took my breath away.

Zave pulled my chair out for me and quipped, "Do I get more brownie points and kisses for being a gentleman again?"

I narrowed my eyes at him as if I was considering what he said with great concentration instead of answering.

He left the room for a moment, and soft jazz floated in the air. He returned and walked toward me, slow and smooth. The man had a nice walk, not a clumsy, clunky walk you would expect from such a big man. He sat across the table, took both of my hands in his, and drew circles on my palms with his thumbs.

"Ms. Frost, I'm waiting for your answer." His intense gaze searched my face.

I could hardly think. His touch seemed to drain my brain. Words were hard. "Umm, what was the question?"

"The first question was...don't you want to kiss me? And the second question was...do I get kisses for brownie points for being a gentleman along with my basket kisses?"

As I looked into his incredibly deep green eyes gleaming in the candlelight, my lips went dry, so I rubbed them together. His eyes focused on my mouth. My cheeks warmed.

"Hello, Mr. Trayce. Here are your appetizers and chilled blue cheese wedge salads. Dinner will be ready shortly." A man dressed in a tuxedo placed the food on the table between us, breaking the hypnotic spell we seemed to be under.

Zave's eyes left my lips and he looked at the man. "Thank you."

The chef bowed low, then left the room to work his magic. Whatever he was making smelled divine. My mouth watered and I licked my lips again.

"You are a dangerous woman, Noelle Frost," Zave

said in a low voice, eyes once again on my lips.

I felt them turn up into a little smile as I looked at him. He was the most handsome man I had ever seen. He reminded me of James Bond. My parents were Double-O-Seven fans, and I felt as if I was looking at my own Sean Connery/James Bond right now—and he was mesmerizing.

"The biggest question is still unanswered. Do you want to kiss me?"

I stared into his eyes. I had no words. My heart flip-flopped. No butterflies now, just plain flip-flops as he stood and gently pulled me to my feet and into his arms. My heart pounded.

We slow-danced around the room, swaying to the jazz rhythm. He held one of my hands, and the other rested lightly on the small of my back. After a few moments, he raised my hand and placed it around his neck. My other hand followed suit. He placed both of his hands on my lower back and pulled me in close so that my cheek lay on his chest. He rested his chin against my forehead. We danced, spellbound, for the rest of the song.

He leaned back and lifted my chin gently. The next song started, slow and smooth. We rocked in place.

"Kiss me, Noelle," he said in a low voice.

I felt a ripple of excitement as he tilted his head down. My eyes drifted closed. His lips met mine, tentative at first, but oh so soft, so warm, so delicious. His mouth was tantalizingly sweet on mine. It was a kiss for my tired and frozen soul to melt into.

"Excuse me. Dinner is served," the waiter announced.

"Thank you and go away," Zave mumbled against

my lips, and then he kissed me again, deeper. Shivers of delight sparked through me. After what seemed way too soon, the kiss ended; Zave placed a soft whisper of a kiss on my nose and then looked at me. "I've wanted to do that ever since our hands touched the day we met at Cuppa Joe's—pretty much within the first minute of seeing you." He cupped my chin and lowered his lips to mine, his kiss tender and light as a summer breeze. Our lips matched perfectly.

We walked arm in arm to our table. I struggled to focus on the food—my senses still reeling from those heavenly kisses.

"Noelle, fourth time's the charm. Did you want to kiss me?" The corner of that luscious mouth turned up.

I loved every minute of this. "Yes, Mr. Xavier Maximillian Trayce, I not only want to kiss you, but I have wondered—no dreamed of—what it would be like for a while," I admitted, surprised at my own brazenness. I realized he might think I was one of those calculating females, so I added, "Don't get me wrong, I haven't been scheming on you because of your basketball...uh...prowess. In truth, the fact that you are a professional athlete is a strike against you. I've had my fill of self-centered, self-absorbed athletes."

Zave's jaw tightened.

I quickly added, "However, I don't think you are a typical egotistical athlete."

His muscles relaxed. A look of relief washed over his face.

I continued, "I'm delighted that you also have a good head on your shoulders and seem to be well grounded. I enjoy being with you. You're a hard-working man with great discipline, which, by the way, is quite impressive. You are kind and good to my sweet Tatum and have brilliant green eyes that…"

I made the mistake of looking into those eyes, which were crinkled up at the corners. He was biting his lip as if not to laugh at me.

"You, beautiful lady, have a tendency to jabber when you're rattled, and my kisses rattled you."

"Oh, you think they did, do you? Well, let me tell you I have been kissed before, and…"

His tall frame leaned over the table and he placed both hands on my cheeks, his lips capturing my lips once again. I felt myself falling, falling, falling—unable to think anymore.

He sat back and chuckled. "You were saying?"

"Okay, I'm done. I'm not saying another word tonight." I tried to pout, but my heart was full, and my lips would do nothing but turn up after those wonderful kisses.

"That's okay. Talk is over-rated anyway. Plus I have yet to collect on my kisses for being a gentleman and making baskets."

"Dream on, big basketball man. You'll get kisses when I'm ready to give you kisses."

"I thought you weren't talking to me any more tonight."

"I'm not, you big lug." This time I did pout.

He laughed. "You're pretty when you pout." He took my hand and kissed it.

"Eat," I ordered.

"Yes, ma'am," he said with a lingering grin. Then he gently set my hand on the table and dug into his dinner.

The food was amazing—heaping bowls of chicken

piccata and shrimp scampi—enough to feed a family of ten. I finished and watched quietly as Zave ate five or six times what I did.

"I've never seen anyone eat so much. How did you do that?"

"I'm just that hungry. I burn through it fast. I always chow down after games." Zave folded his napkin and placed it on the table.

The chef cleared the plates and gave an approving nod to Zave, then asked if we were ready for dessert.

"How about it, Noelle?" he asked me.

"Not yet. I need to let my stomach settle a little first."

"Chef, thank you for a delicious dinner. Why don't you go ahead and close up? Just set the dessert on the table. We'll get to it as soon as we dance and kiss for a while."

I kicked his shin under the table.

He winked at me as the chef grinned, bowed, then disappeared.

Zave stood and extended his hand. "May I have this dance, m' lady?"

He was so charming—my prince charming—I couldn't resist.

He pulled me close. We held each other as we slowly glided around the room. He smelled like fresh limes on a summer breeze. I could stay in his arms forever. I never wanted this to end. My feet seemed to float on a cloud. After five or six way-too-short songs, he led me back to the table, and we enjoyed our dessert of Sogno di Cioccolata, "Chocolate Dream."

"I want to talk with you about something." Zave wiped his mouth with his napkin. Always the gentleman.

"Okay." My heart pounded. I had no idea where this would go.

"My manager mentioned an investment deal that includes you and your Frost Foundation. Tell me a little about it."

I was surprised and once again answered with my great reporter vocabulary. "Really?"

"Yes. I'm interested in what you're doing." The wide-eyed look in his eyes confirmed it.

"Well, it all started with my baby brother, Nicky. He was born with a heart defect. Before he turned two, he died on route to the Children's Hospital in Denver." My voice broke. It was still hard to talk about it. "If there had been a level three children's hospital wing in Colorado Springs, they may have had time to save him."

Zave reached across the table and squeezed both my hands to comfort me.

It worked. I pulled myself together and continued. "My parents set aside the money my dad had inherited from his father and started the Frost Foundation to fund a pediatric wing in our local hospital. After they died..." Another pause and reassuring squeeze. "We four sisters made it our goal to continue where they left off and make sure the Nicholas Charles Frost Pediatric Wing became a reality. We are almost there." I smiled.

"Are you okay if I ask my financial group to look into it? I'm interested in becoming a contributor."

My heart expanded, and I could have danced on a cloud. "I would love it. My sisters and I would love it. Thank you."

He broke out in a huge grin, but in spite of my

excitement, I couldn't stifle a yawn. He checked his watch. "It's three thirteen. Come on, Noelle, I'll take you to your company condo. I think we accomplished a lot on our first official date. Don't you?"

"Yes, our first date and our first kiss. Check those off the list. Right?" I grinned at him.

"Am I just statistics to you?" This time he tried to pout as if he were hurt. His face looked comical with his chin lowered, lips turned down, and his eyes slightly squinted.

Laughing, I stood on my tiptoes and pressed my lips on his as he wrapped his arms around me. There was a sweet taste of chocolate. This was definitely a chocolate fudge kiss.

We finally broke away and I whispered, "No, Zave, you're not a statistic."

I hope you're not too good to be true, that little devil of doubt on my shoulder whispered in my ear.

Chapter Fourteen

I replayed our date over and over until I fell asleep in the soft bed in the corporate condo. I had decided that our first kiss was like velvet—a red velvet cake kiss.

I woke up glowing. When Zave picked me up around eight o'clock the next morning, he looked as happy as I felt. He hugged me, then swung me around and kissed me soundly before putting me back down.

"Good morning, Noelle." His big grin was contagious.

"You know, Zave, I think it's time you call me Elle; all the people I love do."

His head jerked up.

"I mean, you know, all my family and friends call me Elle." I backpedaled.

The corner of his mouth twitched, and then he gave me a quick kiss and said, "Okay, Elle."

We drove to the Springs and picked up Tatum from Holly's.

Holly was tickled to meet Zave. She couldn't stop smiling the entire time we visited. Tatum wanted all Zave's attention, so he excused himself and walked with her to his Jeep as I thanked Holly.

"Are you kidding me, Elle? The man's gorgeous. Did you get that first kiss last night?"

"Shhhhhhh…he'll hear you."

"Well, did you?" I could see she wasn't going to leave it alone.

"Yes." I giggled.

"Woo whooo!" she whooped.

I smacked her arm. "Stop that. He'll know we're talking about him."

"Of course, he will. What else would we be talking about?"

"Mommy, Tree says we're going to Water World." She waved her arm for me to come.

"See you, sis. And...a super big thank you for taking care of Tatum last night." I gave her a hug and ran to the car, afraid she might begin war-whooping again and possibly break into a rain dance.

We stopped by my condo, changed into our swimsuits, and grabbed some towels. Zave took a quick tour and said he loved it.

"I know it's probably tiny compared to where you live, but there's plenty of room for Tatum and me. I love the balcony and our little fenced-in back yard with the swings, playhouse, and garden."

"No, it's perfect and seems nice and safe for you and Tatum." His concern touched my heart.

"You know, Elle." Standing behind me, he wrapped his arms around my waist as we stood on my balcony overlooking the little back yard. "You might be surprised about my apartment. Yes, it's sort of big, but it isn't a home like you have here."

I leaned into him and closed my eyes, sighing. I could get used to him. He felt good in my little world.

"Let's go," shouted Tatum from downstairs.

Reluctantly, I moved out of Zave's warm cocoon of an embrace and took his hand to go.

Water World was a huge indoor water park at the Great Wolf's Lodge. We played in the wave pool, screamed as we slid down each of the ten slides, and roared with laughter when the giant "tipping bucket" dumped its entire load of water on Zave. Once again, Tatum had no fear. She tried everything. There were lots of "Hey, Triple X," and high fives, but for the most part people let us be, as if we were a normal, real family. Tatum had the time of her life as the center of our attention. It was one of the best days ever.

Back at the condo, Tatum and I treated Zave to tacos and our famous home-made Frost salsa. Knowing how Zave ate, we quadrupled the amount of food, and sure enough, there weren't any leftovers.

Tatum got into her pajamas, and we watched a few *Scooby Doo* episodes with her curled up in Zave's lap. I sat next to them under his arm. This was Heaven.

My little angel fell asleep in Zave's arms. We walked side by side while he carried her up the stairs to bed. I definitely could picture him as the kind of "daddy" I wanted for my little girl.

Tatum stirred and opened her eyes. "Tree, read Cinderella, please." I sat on the edge of her bed as Zave folded his large frame into her overstuffed, puffy-pink chair. He looked so out of place I stifled a laugh.

"Once upon a time, there lived a little girl named Cinder-Tatum."

"No, her name is Cinderella." Tatum sat up.

"Oh, sorry. Once upon a time, there lived a little girl named Tater-Rella."

"No, Tree. It's Cinderella." She placed her hands on her hips.

"Okay. Once upon a time, there lived a little girl

named Cinderella."

I watched him read and tease Tatum. This man was the whole package. He was adorable and had an extra sweet spot for my daughter. He was hardworking, kind, patient, caring, understanding, and an incredible kisser. Thinking about his kisses, I tuned out and watched his lips move. "Mmm…luscious."

Both Zave and Tatum looked up at me, surprised.

"Oh no. I said that out loud, didn't I?" I looked back and forth at them as they nodded their heads and grinned.

"Sorry. Go ahead with the story." I tucked my feet up under me and lay back on the pillow by Tatum.

Zave continued to gaze at me for a moment.

I'm sure I my face turned beet red.

He closed the book and said, "The end," leaned over and gave Tatum a kiss on the top of her head. "'Night, Tater Tot." He ruffled her hair.

"'Night, Tree," she said as she pulled up her covers.

I gave her a hug and a kiss and switched off the overhead light.

"I love you, sweetie."

"Love you too, Mom."

Zave reached out his hand, and I took it as he led me back down the stairs. He lit the fireplace, and we settled down on the couch, side by side.

"She's a great kid, Elle. You've done a terrific job." Zave traced the back of my hand with his index finger.

"Thank you. She is pretty wonderful. I don't know what I would have done without her these past few years. She has been my rock, my reason."

"It must have been terribly hard to go through all the things you have. I'm proud of you. You are one tough lady, and pretty, too." He placed his arm around my shoulder and pulled me in close for a soft kiss. "You and Tatum are real. So much about my life is not. I mean, I play games for a living. But when it's all said and done, it's just a game. You and Tatum ground me. You two are a breath of fresh air in my crazy life. Thank you, Elle, for letting me into your world."

I smiled up at him as he lowered his lips to mine. I drank the sweetness of his kiss. His lips were tender and warm. He trailed kisses along my cheek and down the side of my neck, then back again, a series of slow, shivery kisses. His mouth grazed my earlobe. His lips brushed my brow and finished their little exploration, landing back on my lips. The kiss deepened. I needed his kiss like I needed air. These kisses made me whole again. I melted in his arms. This was perfection.

Way too soon, he pulled back, leaving my mouth burning with fire.

"Time for me to go, pretty lady. You are toooo tempting. Tomorrow starts a ten-day road trip, but I'll call you every night, okay?"

"Uh…sure," I managed with my quick use of clever phrases.

He chuckled and I thought—I hoped—he was going to pepper me with more kisses, but instead, he kissed the tip of my nose and grinned as he stood up and backed toward the door.

"'Night, Elle. Lock the door, my lovely lady," he said as he closed the front door, leaving me on the couch dreaming of this wonderful day. The feel of his lips lingered. His kisses were hot and spicy. I think they were jalapeño kisses. I was falling hard for this man.

I pulled a throw over me and watched the fire in deep contentment until a little voice in the corner of my mind couldn't leave it alone and nudged me to be careful. Men are not to be trusted. I pushed the thought back into its cage. Men are human, sometimes good and sometimes bad. Zave is certainly very much a human— and definitely on the good side.

Chapter Fifteen

The morning Zave visited Tatum's school was amazing. He managed to enter the school building without being seen. The students gathered in the gym. I showed up since I wasn't shooting my story until around noon and sat by Tatum on the bleachers.

The principal entered dressed in navy-blue sweatpants and a sky-blue Denver Nuggets jersey over a bright yellow t-shirt. The kids laughed. The laughter turned to cheers and stomping feet when Zave came sprinting into the gym in his team warm-ups. He jogged around, shaking hands here and there, and then stopped in front of Tatum and me. He gave me one of his signature lopsided smiles, melting my heart, and then focused on Tatum.

"Hello, Tatum."

"Hi, Tree." She hopped up and jumped into his arms for a big bear hug.

Zave set her back down and then asked, "Will you please introduce me to your friends?"

Tatum proudly walked over to a boy wearing a Golden State Warriors t-shirt, and a little blonde-headed girl. "Tree, this is Hunter, and this is Cassidy. And guys, this is the Tree. See, I told you he's a giant."

Both of the children had their heads tilted back and their mouths open. I filmed it with my phone camera, sure it would be jiggly because I was laughing so hard.

After shaking their hands, Zave jogged over to a metal frame filled with basketballs and shot around. Every time he swished a basket, which was most of the time, the kids cheered.

The principal chose five sixth graders to play him and Zave. It was hilarious. For the first few minutes Zave toyed with them, letting them get to the basket and pretending that they could guard him. Together he and the principal made an okay team. Then Zave became Triple X and put on a show. He dunked. He juked and dodged the boys. He stole the ball and made shots from half-court. Finally, the sixth graders gave up and group-attacked him each time the ball was in his possession. He dragged them down the court and continued to make baskets.

The students hooted and hollered at all the crazy antics. After a while, Zave's agent blew a whistle, putting a stop to the game.

The principal left the floor huffing and puffing and returned with a microphone for Zave.

The kids gave him their undivided attention. Zave thanked them for letting him visit and then told them a story.

"Once there was a fourth grader who loved basketball, but he was shorter than all the other boys. They made fun of him and wouldn't let him play, so he asked his dad to put up a hoop on the garage. Every day after school, he would eat some delicious cookies or pie his mother made, do his homework, then go outside and shoot baskets. Now notice that I said he did his homework before he shot baskets. That is the most important part of the story."

Zave paused and looked around the gym, then

added slowly, pausing between each word, "Do—your—homework."

The kids groaned.

Zave laughed and said, "The boy decided he'd be the best shooter at his school because it didn't matter how tall you were if you could shoot the ball through the hoop."

"He chose to make one hundred baskets every day before he went to bed. Not just shoot one hundred shots but make one hundred shots. At first it took him about two hours because he missed so many and had to chase down the ball. Sometimes his mom, dad, brothers, or sisters shagged the balls for him, and he would finish in an hour and a half."

Zave walked around looking at the children as he talked.

"After about a year, the boy's shot improved and he could make his one hundred shots in twenty minutes—you know, more shots made and less time chasing the ball. He also played pick-up games with his brothers, sisters, and the neighborhood kids.

"But the boy hadn't grown much taller yet, so he didn't feel ready to try out for the school team." Zave rubbed his chin a moment, thinking, as he walked around.

"His dad put up a light so he could shoot at night. The only time the boy missed shooting his one hundred shots was when his family took vacations. Even then he wadded up papers and shot them into a waste basket, not stopping until he reached one hundred. Sometimes the boy felt tired or discouraged, but he had made a promise to himself, and he chose to keep that promise."

I looked at the students. Few wiggled. They

seemed mesmerized.

Zave continued, "In high school, although still short, he felt good enough about his shooting ability that he decided to try out for the basketball team. Some of the boys laughed at him when he came into the gym." Zave shook his head.

"This time, the boy ignored them. He knew he had worked hard and was ready. His years of practice paid off, and he made the team. The boy continued to complete one hundred shots each and every day and still does to this day. Anyone know who this boy is?" Zave paused and turned slowly around the room.

Some students yelled, "You," and pointed at Zave. Other's yelled, "Triple X."

Zave nodded with a huge grin. When they quieted down, he asked, "What is the most important thing about this story?" He called on a boy with his hand raised.

"To shoot one hundred baskets a day and never give up."

"Good answer, and true. Set a goal and never give up. But there is another point I also want you to remember from this story." He waited and looked around the room.

Finally, Tatum raised her hand.

"Yes, Tatum?"

"To grow up to be a giant and—" She was interrupted by laughter. "—and do your homework," she shouted out over the laughter.

"Exactly. Do your homework!" Zave gave Tatum a thumbs-up.

The principal thanked Zave, and the kids cheered and clapped as he jogged backward out of the gym, waving.

Later that night, Zave came to dinner. He told Tatum how proud he was that she understood his story.

I set the spaghetti down and listened to them discuss how important it was to study, and always do your best, and keep your promises to yourself.

I leaned over and gave Tatum a kiss on the cheek. "I love you, sweetie." Then I walked behind Zave's chair and placed my hands on his shoulders. "Thank you, Zave, for taking time to visit the school today. You were wonderful with the children."

Zave took my hands and pulled me closer. When my head was even with his, he gave me a kiss on the cheek and said, "You are very welcome. I had to meet Cassidy and Hunter. They had never met a giant, you know."

Chapter Sixteen

Zave went on another road-trip. True to his word, he called me every night. If it was an early game, he visited with Tatum too; if not, we talked until it turned into a yawn fest. Talking like this definitely gave us a chance to get to know each other better. We asked each other all kinds of questions and got into some deep subjects.

Much to my relief, we found that we shared the same values, along with many of the same likes and dislikes. We also shared things about our daily lives and laughed a lot. I had no idea there was anyone out there like him. Hope for a strong, healthy relationship with a good man burned brightly in my heart.

It was Saturday once again, and almost time for work. Ready early, I took the extra time to do some research on my uncle, Simon. His name popped up connecting him to a number of businesses, but nothing shady came to light. I shrugged my shoulders. He must be okay. Maybe I should let it go. It seemed time for me to be more open to giving men a chance and that included Zave and Simon. Glancing at the clock, I closed my laptop, gathered my keys, and hurried out the door with Tatum.

At Joy's house, I gave Tatum a hug good-bye. "See you later this afternoon, sweetie."

"Joy, thanks once again for tending Saturdays.

Love you, sis."

"Love you more. Now go to work already. We have the Vog to battle today." Joy grinned as her caped and hooded Batman boys ran into the kitchen, grabbed Tatum's arm, and escaped into the family room with her.

I giggled as I climbed into the car. The warm Colorado sun and beautiful autumn leaves celebrated a lovely day with me. How lucky to have my sisters. The sometimes strange hours my job required would be almost impossible without them. It really did take a village to raise a child, and I was so blessed to have my "Village Sisters." I laughed at my own dorky humor. Life was certainly looking up.

****

"This is Noelle Frost, CBS 4, Denver. Now back to you at the station, Jacob." I continued to smile into the camera until the cameraman said, "That's a wrap."

"Thanks, Freddy. See you back at work next week."

"Sure thing, Noelle," he said as he packed up his equipment.

We were outside Schmidt's Jewelry for this last shot. A small crowd had gathered. A man at the side had a familiar stance. My heart jolted. He looked like Dad. Same height, same frame, same smile. Then I realized it was Simon.

He maneuvered his way to me. "I saw the CBS 4 camera van and thought I might find you here working." He sounded apologetic and a little sheepish.

I clasped my hands behind my back.

"May I buy you lunch?" Simon shoved his hands into his pockets like an unsure teenager.

"No, thank you. I have plans," I answered with reserve. I still wasn't sure what he was doing here in Colorado Springs...or who he really was. Although I was working on the trust factor, I wasn't quite ready to give him a giant welcome back to the family yet.

"Another time, perhaps." He clenched his jaw, turned, and strolled away.

Watching him, I realized my gut instinct told me to keep an eye on him. He may turn out to be the best uncle in the world, and if he did, great, especially for sweet Chrissy. She already looked up to him as kind of a surrogate father figure. But I needed to give it a little more time.

Then it hit me. I was beginning to listen to myself, even stand up for myself and trust my own judgement once again. It had been a long time coming. Blake had been so emotionally abusive that it had twisted my thinking and reasoning so that I didn't know who I was anymore.

With a little "proud of myself" nod, I walked back into the jewelry store.

"Mr. Schmidt, thanks for letting me cover the theft and return of that incredible tiara. You came across well on the camera, and it's great to cover a story with a happy ending."

"You're most welcome, Ms. Frost. I'm pleased to have it back." The elderly gentleman smiled warmly.

"I've never seen a real diamond tiara. It's so incredibly beautiful. That thief certainly has great taste."

Mr. Schmidt leaned against the counter with a twinkle in his eye and asked, "Would you like to try it on?"

"Really? May I?" I hardly dared to even touch it. He held it out to me.

I accepted it with both hands. The white gold frame felt sturdy, but light. The two hundred half-carat diamonds glittered like their own galaxy. I moved in front of the antique oval mirror on the glass counter and carefully set the tiara on my head.

A wave of sheer pleasure rushed through me as I stared at my reflection. I'd always wanted to grow up to be a princess, a mermaid, or a fairy. This was beyond fun, to see this elegant five-million-dollar diamond-laden masterpiece on my head.

I admired the tiara from a few different angles, then took several deep breaths and let out a sigh as I carefully removed it and handed it back to the owner.

"Thank you. That was a thrill of a lifetime. Maybe a bucket list item that I never would have hoped was possible." Being a reporter could be so much fun. I flashed my TV smile at him, dimples and all.

"You're welcome. It's nice to see it on such a pretty young lady. It's often rented by celebrities for special events, but it has never looked so lovely."

"Why, thank you, kind sir." I did a little curtsy and we both laughed.

The door chimed. A tall, ginger-haired young woman dressed in tight clothing and high heels sashayed across the room toward us.

I recognized her as the daughter of the owner of the Denver Nuggets, Rhonda Santori, the one who'd hung all over Zave not too long ago. My stomach tightened, and I found my arms crossing involuntarily.

"Hello." Mr. Schmidt turned toward her. "May I help you?"

"I was driving by and saw the TV news truck outside. Is there a big sale I should know about?" She gave me a sideways glance.

I stepped away to let the owner do his thing. I certainly didn't want to talk to her.

Mr. Schmidt smiled. "No particular sale other than the usual great value on our jewelry, madam. Is there something in particular you'd like…a new set of earrings or a lovely necklace?"

"Maybe, but I think I'll just look around. I'll let you know if I need some help." She waved him off with her hand and then looked into the nearest glass cabinet.

I decided this was a good time to leave. She looked up as I tried to walk around her. "Oh, it's you, the reporter lady—funny running into you here. I believe you know my boyfriend, the basketball player, Triple X."

"I know Zave." My lips tightened.

"He's coming home Wednesday night. We're having a special private dinner. I thought I would look around this place." She waved her hand in the air. "I mean, it's as good as any other jewelry store to look at engagement rings, don't you think?"

The look in her squinting eyes was sheer spite.

"Well…" I cleared my throat. "Yes, this is a lovely store." I cringed as my word skills once again failed me.

She stuck out her hand. "Let me introduce myself. I'm Rhonda Santori."

I guess I looked at her hand for a moment too long. She shoved her hand closer to me. I reached out and took it. She shook like a limp fish.

"I'm Noelle Frost," I said as I rubbed my right

hand on my skirt.

"Of course you are. I'm glad I ran into you today. There's this rumor going around that you have taken an interest in my man." Her smiling mouth looked more like a sneer.

Wow, the woman wasted no time attacking. I didn't say anything. I wasn't surprised by rumors. I had heard plenty about Zave before and now that we were dating. Most of it had no basis or was so far off the mark it was laughable. I stood still, staring at her.

"Caught, are you? Well, listen to me, and listen good. Triple X belongs to me. My father owns him, and soon I will, too. He's quite scrumptious, isn't he? Like I said, I'll pick him up from the airport Wednesday, and we'll be having a private dinner—extremely private. I bought the most slinky, red dress—fits me perfectly." She giggled and looked down at her skimpily dressed body.

Her attire left little to the imagination. I had to admit she looked pretty darn perfect. My stomach now ached as the tension buzzed around us.

"I'm sure he won't be able to take his eyes off of me." Rhonda smirked. "I expect to be engaged by the end of the evening." She pinned me with her cold eyes.

Alarm shot through me. I had to get out of there, now. I turned away and wanted to run, but I forced myself to walk to maintain some dignity, although I walked fast.

I jumped into my car and looked back at the store. "Good, she didn't follow me," I spoke to the windshield.

I grabbed the steering wheel and squeezed it hard for a minute until I felt calm enough to drive. I figured I might run into her someday but was surprised how much venom she'd spewed. Zave was right. She was one determined lady.

A knock on my window made me jump. Rhonda peered in. She couldn't possibly have any more poison to shoot at me. I rolled down the window.

She had a cell phone to her ear and spoke in a syrupy voice, "Yeah, X, dinner is going to be so nice— just you and me, baby, all alone. Wait 'till you see my red dress I told you about," she oozed. "Uh huh, me too. I'm so glad you dumped that clinging little fan girl from the TV. Yeah, I know, I know. She was nothing but a passing fling." She laughed. "I can't wait to pick you up from the airport, lover boy." She turned away for a moment, holding the phone with both hands and talking softly.

I clamped my eyes closed. I assumed she was saying a few choice things that weren't appropriate. I took what I hoped was a calming breath, then opened my eyes to see that she had turned back around and looked directly at me with a wicked grin. She lowered her phone and pushed something. She must have put it on speaker phone.

"X, baby, I have someone who wants to talk to you."

I didn't think I could stomach much more.

I pressed the window button but stopped halfway when I heard Zave's unmistakable voice say, "Hold on, Rhonda, I want to talk to you."

Rhonda laughed then said, "I know, baby. I want to talk to you some more, too. Let me call you right back. Bye." Then she let out the most ridiculous, shrill, disgusting giggle.

I stared at her in shock.

She stuffed her phone inside the top of her skin-tight blouse. "See? I told you. Stay away, Noelle. He's taken. He's been playing you. You see, he's a player like me, but at least he's my player." She snarled at me.

Stunned, almost unable to breathe, I rolled the window up and started the car. She stepped aside as I backed out and drove away.

This made no sense. Why was she saying those things to Zave on the phone? Zave getting engaged on Wednesday—no way. I knew he was flying in late Wednesday, but he'd told me he had a dinner with the owner of the team, so he would see me Thursday.

"Oh, my gosh. He had dinner with the owner of the team which could easily include his daughter—or was it in reality dinner with just his daughter? It's true," I voiced out loud. A sword cut through my heart. The pain was deep and real.

Then anger flared. I squeezed the steering wheel so tight, my knuckles turned white. He said he wasn't interested in her. He said he wanted to stick around and spend time with me…and Tatum. He said we grounded him and were a breath of fresh air in his crazy life. We made him happy.

It was Blake all over again. I thought Zave was different. He didn't have any signs of being abusive like Blake, but the past image of Blake and his mistress together in the hot tub flashed through my mind. My stomach and eyes burned.

I thought I had finally broken the pattern. I'd met a nice guy and was beginning to trust him.

What an idiot I was. I smashed the steering wheel with one fist.

I didn't have much faith in men and had tried to be cautious with Zave, had tried to keep him out of my heart, but he was so charming. No, it wasn't just that. He seemed so sincere. He seemed so kind, so real, so considerate. I had believed him when he said he cared about me—that he cared about Tatum. I mean, he even talked to Tatum through the TV. He knew rumors would start from that interview, but he didn't care.

He didn't act like a player with Tatum and me. I had to admit that up until now, I thought Zave had the qualities that would make him a great husband and companion and a wonderful dad. Tatum seemed to think he was super. Oh, how I wished he hadn't turned out like all the rest of them. A moan escaped my throat.

Now I knew different. Hope died in that moment I overheard Zave saying he wanted to talk to Rhonda.

Then the thought hit me that something must be wrong with me to keep allowing myself to get duped by these smooth-talking athletes. I must have gullible written on my forehead. Other women realized when they were being played, and they got out quickly, but maybe I'd ignored the signs because I craved love. Maybe I needed validation that I was loveable. For a reporter, one who bases life on facts, I sure was living in la-la land with my fairy tale version of romance. My version of love was just that—make-believe.

Sure, I knew there were women young and old, here and on road trips, who threw themselves at him. That went with the territory. But he said he wasn't interested and wanted a wife and family. I had swallowed the nice guy act hook, line, and sinker.

Tears ran down my cheeks. I continued trying to work through this and realized every man had temptations, whether at work in an office, driving a truck, wearing a police uniform, CEO to ditch digger...or playing sports for a living. There were always women around. But good men weren't interested in other women, no matter what. Dad had loved Mom, always, and now forever. There had to be more good men like my father. I believed now I would never find one.

My heart broke. I rubbed my chest with the heel of my palm.

I had to get off the road. I pulled into a convenience store parking lot. I slumped in my seat, then dropped my head into my hands and sobbed.

It hurt. It hurt so much, too much for six weeks of knowing someone. I was such a fool. Once again, I'd almost fallen for a jock. "Oh, stop kidding yourself, Elle. You fell down the Grand Canyon for this guy," I croaked out loud.

I cried hard for a long time, until the sobs turned into ragged breathing.

I gave myself a pep talk to try to pull myself together. "Look at the bright side, Elle. You could never have handled all the women he met anyway. You weren't cut out for that kind of life. This was probably for the best—especially before he got any closer to Tatum.

"Your sisters tried to warn you. You tried to be cautious. You were blinded by chemistry and that adorable lopsided smile..."

My bravado slipped and my heart did some slow, sad beats as a fresh batch of tears flowed.

"Oh, Mom, I wish you were here to talk to. You would help me get through this and..." I broke down into loud sobs again.

It took me at least a half hour to pull myself together once again.

"Stop it, Elle. You're done crying." I wiped my face and blew my nose and looked into the rear-view mirror. My eyes were puffy—my face streaked with mascara. I was a mess. I stared into the mirror.

"Well, he's gone. Out of my life. Rhonda can have him," I shouted as I smacked the steering wheel with both hands.

Tatum and I didn't need a man to be happy. That much I knew for sure. I made a good living, and Tatum and I had everything we needed.

He was like the rest of them, and I would tell him that tonight when—or—if he called after his game. What was I thinking? I sobbed. He wouldn't dare call tonight.

"Now how am I going to get past Joy to pick up Tatum?" I needed a little more time before I could face her. I'd better call.

"Hello, Joy. I'm running a little late. Are you guys okay if I get there in a half hour or so?"

"Sure. I ordered pizza, and I'm not sure Tatum would let you take her before she ate some, anyway."

I let out a sniff.

"Are you okay?" Joy's voice sounded concerned.

"Sure. Maybe I'm coming down with a bit of a cold. No worries, though. I'll be fine. You know me. Got to go. See you soon." I hung up before she could question me any further.

Chapter Seventeen

I picked up Tatum, but not without a few questions from Joy. She knew something was up but had the good sense to not ask much in front of the kids. I was sure she'd call later after Tatum and her boys were asleep.

I listened to Tatum's excited chatter all the way home about defeating the Vog with her cousins. Grateful I didn't need to talk, my mind wandered.

Family…I'd lost my wonderful parents, my sweet little brother, too. Tatum would never know them, but we both had my three sisters and my three nephews. They were incredible. None of us needed a man in our family circle.

I spent extra time reading and snuggling Tatum that night. The phone rang several times, but I ignored it, sure it was Joy wanting to know what was going on. I wasn't ready to talk to her yet.

"Mommy? Can I talk to Tree tonight?" Tatum wiggled a little closer.

"No, sweetie. I'm not sure if we can talk to him. Tree is out of town until Wednesday. He has lots of basketball games to play and is so busy." My eyes watered. Stop it, Elle. No crying in front of Tatum. She doesn't deserve to be wrapped up in this mess. I need to do a better job of protecting her.

The phone's incessant ringing woke me. I had been so emotionally exhausted I had fallen asleep beside my little angel and for a short while had found some peace. It was time to face my sister's questions.

"Hello." My voice cracked. Darn, I had wanted to start out strong.

"Hi, Elle. I called a couple of times tonight, but you didn't answer. What gives?" Joy sounded worried.

"Not much, and I'm so tired, sis. Can we talk about it at the Mason Jar Friday? It's really no big deal."

"It's that Triple X guy, isn't it? He hurt you, didn't he?" She sounded angry.

"Well, yes…umm…yes, he did. Look, you guys were right. He's just another typical basketball player, and I mean 'player.' He has a girlfriend, and silly me, I thought it was me, so congratulations. You were right once again. I'm no good at picking guys."

I knew I sounded bitter and was being a little snarky toward her, but I was too tired and hurt to filter the pain. I wanted to go back to sleep and for this to go away.

Joy was quiet for a moment and then spoke softly as she said, "Listen, Elle, I didn't want to be right. None of us did. We love you and want you to be happy, so we got a little overprotective. I know you need some time to process what happened. But I'm here. So are Holly and Chrissy. When you are ready to talk or cry, I have a soft shoulder with your name on it."

"Thank you. I'm sorry. I didn't mean to snap at you. It's just so hard. I keep doing this over and over again. Will I ever learn?" I let out a little groan.

"Sure you will. I'm proud that you opened up and at least gave someone a chance. That tells me you're beginning to heal and even trust yourself a little." She paused and took a deep breath. "And, honey, we all strike out more often than not—even most baseball players strike out more than they hit."

Her voice sounded so soothing. She was right. At least I had a little faith in men, enough to try. I'd been strong enough to step out of my comfort zone and open my heart. I had to give myself some credit that I was finally healing from that horrible marriage.

For so long I had been convinced that Blake's abuse was my fault, but no more. I knew he owned his actions, not me. Women did not cause men to be abusive. Abusers managed that evil all by themselves.

I knew I deserved an honest and good man, one who didn't take his nasty temper or frustrations out on me—a man who didn't cheat. I felt a little peace, and a small smile crept onto my face, and then I yawned.

"I heard that. You get some sleep, and I'll see you and Tatum at church tomorrow. In fact, why don't you two have dinner with me and the boys...all my boys. Sean is coming with his son."

I let out a sigh.

"I didn't mean to—"

"No, no. It's fine. We'd love to come. I can whip up a cake in the morning for dessert." I yawned again. This was good. Talking to her helped. I realized I just might live. "Thanks, Joy, for being there."

"Where else would I be? See you tomorrow, my brave sister. I love you." Joy always knew what to say to comfort us younger sisters.

"Love you more, and thanks." I smiled and hung up.

I gave Tatum one last kiss on her forehead and quickly changed into my PJs. I snuggled into my pillows and pulled my covers up high under my chin.

The phone rang again. The little bit of encouragement and peace I had found talking to Joy flew out into the dark night.

"Hello." Again my voice almost broke.

"Hi, Elle. Wow, I missed you today. I bought you and Tatum surprises. I can't wait to get back and give them to you both."

I remained quiet. He sounded so good, so normal, so sweet.

"Elle? Are you there?"

"Yes, Zave, I'm here." My voice became stronger.

"What's wrong?" He sounded truly concerned.

Oh, he was good.

"Wrong? Be decent and do me one favor, just one. Don't play me anymore. I'm not like the others. This is over. Don't call me or talk to Tatum through the TV anymore. Leave us alone. Goodbye, Xavier Trayce."

As I pulled the phone away from my ear, I heard, "Elle, Elle, wait. Let's talk about this. Elle…"

Click.

Done.

My stomach twisted and churned. I collapsed in a heap on my bed.

Chapter Eighteen

I sat at my desk at the TV station in Denver, lost in thought. A week had gone by since I'd told Zave goodbye. Several pictures had appeared in the news. Photos of Zave with Rhonda either clinging to his arm staring up at him with an adoring puppy-dog-look or standing nearby in the background of one of his after-game interviews. He had called and texted me numerous times. I finally blocked his number and erased the voice messages without listening to them. My heart couldn't take any more of this. I didn't want to be played any more, and it was over. I didn't trust men, and I certainly didn't trust him.

Tatum asked about him, but I always told her he had basketball games to play and was a very busy man. I assured her each time that she and I were a team of our own and then distracted her with other things.

One night at bedtime, she asked how come he didn't call her anymore. A lump rose in my throat, and I snuggled her close as I scrambled for something to say that was true but wouldn't break her heart…like mine. Finally, I said, "You know, Tatum, Tree is a very famous man and has many people all around him and has so many things to do. I think he got too busy." The voice in my head added, "He's too busy with somebody else, not us."

"Noelle? Mel wants to see you." I shook my head

to clear it from my sad thoughts and looked up at Freddy as he stumbled by my desk carrying a load of camera equipment.

"Thanks, Freddy." Good. I needed a new assignment to take my mind off Zave.

****

"You want me to what?" I asked incredulously. My heart pounded and I fisted my hands. "Mel—um, I don't—uh, cover the big sports stories in Denver." I stopped talking. I knew I was rambling.

Mel looked at me in surprise. I had never hesitated accepting a story assignment before.

"Look, I know it's a Friday night, so yes, it would be overtime, but Mandy has pneumonia and won't be able to be part of the 'Andy and Mandy Sports Team.' You're my best reporter, so I'm giving you the opportunity." Mel gave me his sweet, grandfatherly smile of encouragement.

"But I haven't ever covered sports. I mean, I'm not really a sports reporter." The thought of having to cover the Denver Nuggets game…which meant being in the reporting spotlight around Triple X's huge spotlight, made my stomach quake.

"Look, Noelle. You're a reporter. Reporters report. You know how to do that, and you do it well. Just enjoy the game and then report." Mel's voice had changed to his "I'm the boss" voice that booked no argument.

"You and Andy have seats in the second row, center court. Relax and look at it as the plum assignment it is. I know you'll do great. Thank you, and…you're welcome." Mel turned and walked back into his office.

He must have thought it was nerves. He was only

partly right. It was nerves, stomach, head, and heart.

All week long I dreaded Friday, which of course, made it come faster. I had reserved the corporate condo in case I was too exhausted to drive home. I dropped Tatum off at Joy's for the night.

Joy gave me a long hug, almost bringing me to tears again, and told me to hang in there. We Frost ladies were tough, and I would get through this night.

As I drove to Denver, my stomach knotted up every time I thought of seeing Zave. I figured watching him play was going to be rough. I knew that more often than not he was interviewed after the game. I planned to maneuver it so that Andy did that interview. It was too soon to come face to face with that man. I always felt better in tough situations when I had a plan, so now I had my plan and decided I could make it work.

Mel had given me Saturday off, since I was covering the game Friday night. I forced myself to change gears and focused on the fun things Tatum and I had scheduled for tomorrow after her gymnastics.

Images of Zave kept popping into my mind in spite of my efforts to block them out.

"Go away." I ordered him out of my head. Another happy Zave memory showed itself, and I gave up. It was going to be a rough night.

I met Andy at the station, and we took a CBS 4 vehicle. I sat quietly as we drove and wasn't good company, but Andy didn't seem to mind.

He loved sports, especially basketball, so he talked about who was favored to win and which player would match up best with players on the opposing team. The stats this man knew were mind-boggling.

I was grateful for his chatter.

We made our way to our seats, greeting a few other reporters on the way. There was Verlayne Sample, the blue-haired Denver Nuggets' most fanatical fan.

She squealed when she saw me and gave me a big squeeze. She asked me something, probably about how Zave and I were doing, but I couldn't hear her over the music blasting from the sound system in the jumbotron up in the highest reaches of the Pepsi Center.

I slumped in my seat and pretended to read the program as my stomach throbbed in rhythm to music. A picture caught my eye; there was Zave, grinning into the camera, his green eyes even more brilliant because of his flushed face. He looked so good. My heart pounded in my chest.

I couldn't keep beating myself up for falling for this guy. Any woman would. Next time I thought I was starting to like a guy, I'd hire an investigator first thing, to see if he is a no-good cheater. Yes, that's what I'd do. Good, I had a plan. I was now going to sit up and enjoy the game, like my boss told me to.

The lights dimmed. My heel bounced up and down on the floor, and I clutched my hands tight.

The crowd roared and stomped their feet. It was time for the team to make their Hollywood-like entrance. The disco-mirrored ball reflected streaks of light around the cavernous arena as the players jogged out of their tunnel.

As much as I tried to avoid it, my eyes searched until they found number thirteen. The memory of him telling me, "I wanted to kiss you from the first moment I saw you on August thirteenth," brought a new dagger slash to my heart.

"Stop it, Elle. No more thinking about stuff like

that," I scolded myself. No one around seemed to notice.

Zave, in the flesh, stood about twenty feet away. It was dark in the stands so I was sure he couldn't see me. I was torn between sadness and sweet memories. Sitting there was so much like that night I'd gone to his game, followed by dinner, dancing, and...kissing. It had been amazing to spend time with him. I'd really felt that he was different.

"Put it aside, Elle." I said out loud. "Enjoy the game," I repeated over and over again as I wrung my hands.

"What are you saying, Noelle?" Andy hollered over the noise.

"Oh, nothing." I smiled at him.

A local high school band played "The Star-Spangled Banner."

Zave stood at attention with his hand over his heart. He'd told me how much he loved our country and one of his favorite things about the games was the chance to honor our flag at the beginning. That had added to all the things I admired about him.

A lump grew in my throat, and an unwanted tear escaped down my cheek. I had wanted him to be the one.

After the cheers, the full arena lights went up. I watched him run onto the floor when the announcer boomed the starters' names. The crowd went wild chanting, "X, X, X, X..."

"Keep it together, Elle. He can't see you. He'll be focused on the game," I assured myself out loud. Just in case, I leaned back in my seat and placed my large, purple floppy purse on my lap in an attempt to protect my heart. I opened my program and peeked over the top.

"Snow cones," a vender hollered from the aisle.

"Want one?" Andy turned to me.

"Sure. Half cherry, half blue raspberry, please." My comfort food, and I sure needed comfort right now. Plus eating one would help hide my face.

"You want two?" Andy looked confused.

"No, one—half cherry, half blue raspberry." I grinned at him like it was normal.

"Okey-dokey." Andy called out my order and then a grape one for himself.

"Here you go, Noelle. Isn't this the greatest job in the world, sitting here eating snow cones and watching the Nuggets play?" Andy was like a little kid on Christmas Day.

"Uhh…yup," was all I could think of as a reply— always the articulate reporter. No way was I going to tell Andy that I was uncomfortable being here and scared that Zave might see me.

The tip-off went to the Nuggets, so the cheering stopped any more discussion, thank goodness. I lowered the program and kept nibbling on my snow cone, keeping it in front of my face. The teams ran up and down the court, trading baskets back and forth, and Zave had a great game, as usual.

At halftime, Andy turned to me, looking animated. "Can you believe Triple X? Man, the way he's playing tonight. It looks like he's in the ballpark for another triple-double." Andy slapped me on the shoulder like I was one of the guys.

"He is amazing." My heart sank. I didn't want to spend halftime talking about Zave, so I excused myself for a restroom visit.

I took my time and returned about a minute into the third quarter to see Zave swish another three, putting the Nuggets ahead by ten. The crowd went wild. I had to admit, even though my heart ached, it was amazing to see such a gifted athlete perform. Zave moved so smoothly out on the floor and made those three-pointers look like he could sink them in his sleep.

The crowd roared again.

"Did you see that steal? Can you believe it? Triple X hits a three and then steals the ball. Here he comes. He's gonna dunk it!" Andy jumped to his feet, as did everyone around us.

I couldn't see, so I stood up and leaned to the right of the guy in the front row.

Zave was dribbling down the court. He glanced around to see where the opposing team members were, and our eyes met. A zing zapped through me as Zave's gaze penetrated deep into my soul. I froze.

He must have lost focus on the ball because it bounced to the side and out of bounds. He slowed to a jog as he continued the dribbling motion, bouncing the empty air. The ref blew his whistle. The crowd went silent for the first time all night.

Zave stopped moving but continued to stare at me as his teammates walked toward him. Most of them had their arms stretched out as if to ask, Where's your head, bro?

Zave snapped out of it, releasing my eyes. My knees gave out and I dropped back into my seat, stunned, my heart pounding a million beats a minute. Whatever we had between us was still powerful, regardless of the break-up.

The coach sent in a sub, and Zave walked back to his seat without looking at me. I couldn't blame him. I mean, I'd broken up with him without telling him the reason or giving him the chance to confirm or deny it. I'd shut him out by avoiding his calls and texts—very grown up of me.

My protective side reared its head again, and I thought, what was there to tell? He was a player and he played me and…I wouldn't be played anymore.

An usher reached between the two fans in front of me and handed me a note. Andy leaned over my shoulder to read it with me.

My fingers trembled as I opened it up.

Noelle,

We need to talk after the game.

Things are not always as they seem.

Zave

Things were not always as they seemed. Sure, but that didn't make any sense here. I'd heard his voice on the phone with Rhonda in that horrible call, loud and clear.

"Is that from Triple X?" Andy interrupted me, sounding excited.

I folded the note and dropped it into my bag, stalling for an answer. "Umm, well, I guess we'll find out, won't we?" Good, Elle, real clever answer—I guess we'll find out. I certainly didn't want Andy around if—and that was a big if—I decided to talk to Zave.

I fidgeted throughout the rest of the game as it went by in a blur.

Zave seemed out of focus. His timing off. He threw up bricks, turned the ball over, and his passing was almost comical.

The other players fed off Zave's poor performance on the court. The Nuggets looked more like a college team in the final quarter instead of the number one pro team in the world. For the first time in weeks, the Nuggets lost. The crowd seemed stunned. Many of them left before the final buzzer.

As a fan, I felt bad, too, but it was time to go to work. I wanted to do the interviews and get out of there fast.

"Hey, Noelle, since Triple X wants to talk to you anyway, why don't you do the interview with him?"

I panicked. Sweat trickled down my back. "Why don't I do an interview with the sixth man, Carmichael? I made a few notes when he came off the bench. He was one of the few bright spots of the game."

"Mandy and I usually fight over who gets to interview Triple X, and here I am being a gentleman, offering you the prime interview. Come on, Noelle, take it. You may never get a chance to talk to a superstar again." Andy winked at me and climbed over the front row seat.

"Wait," I called after him, my heart racing. Apparently, Andy couldn't hear me above the noise of the crowd moving out of the building.

"You go talk to that boy," said an exasperated-sounding voice to my right.

I turned to see a head of blue hair attached to Verlayne Sample, the little elderly uber fan.

She took my arm and scolded, "Young lady. You lost us a game tonight. Whatever you let get between you and your man, you go work it out with him and set the Nuggets' world right. I don't want any more games lost. You hear?"

My mouth hung open in surprise.

Verlayne reached up and actually pushed my jaw closed before I could reply, and added, "Go on now. Go talk to him. He's over there." She shoved me onto the basketball court.

For a little old lady, she had a lot of spunk and some strong arms.

Freddy, the cameraman, appeared at my side. "Come on, Noelle, we need to catch Triple X before he heads into the locker room."

I sighed. "Well, I guess I'm talking to Zave after all," I said to nobody in particular.

We wound our way through the crowd on the court to the one man I wasn't ready to face.

My heart dropped to the floor. My voice shook as I stood before him. "Xavier, a tough game. What happened here tonight?" I purposely didn't use his nickname, Zave, or even Triple X. That was for friends and fans, and I was no longer either one of them. I managed to hide my emotions and set my face to neutral for the camera as I raised the microphone up close to his lips—those soft, sexy lips. "Stop it right now, Elle." I murmured to myself, rattled.

"Stop it? Don't you want me to answer your question?" Zave looked at me with a twinkle in his eye.

"Yes, of course." This time I glared at him.

His face broke into a huge smile as he said, "It wasn't our night. I think, overall, our concentration was off."

"You seem pretty happy for having your first loss of the season." I looked at his chin—I couldn't handle seeing that wonderful smile up close.

"You win some, you lose some. That's all part of basketball. You have to be able to let things roll off and continue to believe. Things aren't always as bad as they seem. We'll be ready for our game tomorrow night. Next time I hope to have my lucky charm on my side," he said in a cheerful voice, matching his big smile.

"A lucky charm? What is that?"

I held the mic close to him again. "It's my favorite person in the whole world, Noelle Frost." His grin continued.

I looked at him with eyes narrowed, but a good reporter follows a lead.

"And who is your favorite person in the whole world?" I challenged him, then took a deep breath and braced myself for the moment of complete truth with this man. My self-talk kicked in. Pull it together, Elle. Be professional. If he says "Rhonda," then ask about the rumor of them being engaged. Maybe I could get something positive out of this, like a scoop on the wedding date...if I didn't lose it and start crying on camera.

"Noelle."

"Yes, Xavier?"

"Who's on first..." Zave chuckled, then lowered his voice and spoke quietly, "I just told you. My lucky charm is you, Noelle." His smile went soft. He looked at me as if the camera didn't exist anymore.

I stared at him.

"Look, Noelle, you have to listen to me now. I'm not engaged to anyone. There isn't anyone else. I know someone told you different, but that's the truth. Okay...there is another little lady, named Tatum, who I'm crazy about, but I think you'll agree that she's too charming for her own good."

As usual, I was full of words of wisdom and stared at him with my mouth open, ready to catch passing flies.

Zave leaned closer and said, "Noelle, I need you both in my life." His look was so intent, I almost took a step backward.

"Uh, we're broadcasting live. You do know that, don't you?" I managed to ask as my knees wobbled and those dog-gone butterflies made their way around my stomach as if they were racing in Monte Carlo.

"Yes. And if this is what it takes for you to hear me and believe me, then so be it. You're a reporter, and now you got your scoop. I'm hoping this is a win/win situation."

And then that handsome, charming giant of a man leaned down and planted an earth-shattering kiss on my lips for the whole world to see. I forgot everything else and dropped the mic.

Chapter Nineteen

That kiss of all kisses finally had to end. If Zave hadn't whisked me off into the team tunnel, I think I might have melted onto the basketball court.

"I'm going to take a quick shower," he said. "Please, please, say you'll wait for me." Another sparkling grin jumped out at me.

"Yes." I laughed.

"Good—no, great!" He punched the air. "Jordan, will you please take Ms. Frost up to the Team Box and help her avoid any fans hanging around?"

"Will do, Triple X. This way, Ms. Frost." The man looked delighted to be asked to help us as he motioned me toward the elevator.

We managed to enter the box without being interrupted by anyone. There were at least thirty soft seats facing the glass wall overlooking the court. Rhonda was out on the balcony talking to an extremely tall young man. I knew that the Nuggets often brought in recruits and treated them to a game or two in the corporate box as part of wooing new players. He must be one of them. Rhonda laughed at something he said and flipped her hair with her fingers. Looked like Rhonda had moved on to another victim, the poor guy. I stayed inside the glass walls and sat down in the back corner where I was sure they couldn't see me.

I couldn't believe Zave had just done that on air.

My whole body tingled and the huge cloud of doom and gloom that had trailed me since we broke up evaporated with that one delicious kiss. I touched my lips. They were still warm and tasted a bit salty, yet sweet. It was a kettle corn kiss.

This kind of thing had never happened to me. I was Cinderella—no—Noella or Ellerella, I thought as a giggle spilled out. So, this was what it felt like to be a princess, to win the lottery in love, to finally have someone I could believe in and share with. I felt flushed and never wanted to stop grinning. Good thing most of the people in the box were gone and the few who remained weren't looking my way.

Zave was known to keep his private life private. He would never, ever do something like that in front of the television cameras unless he meant it. I had no doubt that he meant every word he said. He'd taken a big risk out there. I couldn't even imagine what would have happened if I had pushed him away or stormed off in the middle of the interview.

That would have been horrid, lonely, sad, and an absolute tragedy. I'd been so caught up in my own story, my strong distrust, and had been wrong all along. I'd let the damaged part of me taint my thoughts. No more. I was ready to allow myself to let this happiness take me on an incredible journey. "This must be what it's like to float on a cloud, win the golden ticket, take the world championship, live happily ever after," I whispered.

I don't think my grin had gone away since that magnificent kiss—that kiss that a good million or more people witnessed, I thought, laughing.

A high-pitched giggle from Rhonda interrupted my

thoughts. I watched her as she ran her fingers up the young man's arm.

"Yuck." Rhonda, Rhonda. I should have talked to Zave. There would always be Rhondas, or ladies like that homewrecker, Cherise, who chased men and didn't care who they hurt. It took two people to have integrity, to remain faithful in a relationship, to make it work. Zave's declaration before the world tonight showed him to be a man of integrity, if not a little crazy, and now I needed to show faith in him.

I'd let Rhonda get to me because of my own paranoia and fear after the betrayal and cruelty I had lived through during my former marriage. I vowed to move forward and face those fears and realize that not all men were wired to be or chose to be abusive. My own father was never that way. Joy's husband was never that way. Some of my friends and co-workers seemed to have great marriages and relationships. Zave's bold move tonight had saved me from sabotaging the best thing—no, the best man ever for me, and Tatum, too.

Tatum—oh no—Tatum may have seen that. I was sure Joy did and had called Holly and Chrissy by now. I'd better talk to them. I made a group call and only managed to get in a few words with all of their whooping and teasing. All three of them had seen the interview.

Joy did manage to tell me that Tatum had fallen asleep before the end of the game. She said she'd let me share my news and show her the video clip myself but cautioned me to do it before the weekend was over, so the story didn't come from kids or teachers at school.

A peaceful warmth surrounded me. I took some

slow breaths and thought about my parents, wishing they could have met Zave. They would have liked him.

I heard the door behind me open and there he was. Zave glanced around the empty room, looking worried, until his eyes met mine.

"Oh good. For a minute, I thought I'd imagined the last half hour." With long strides he reached me in a few seconds. He pulled me up and into a big bear hug. We clung to each other for what seemed like eternity but was definitely eons too short.

He whispered in my ear, "Do you forgive me for the on-air stunt I pulled?"

I leaned back to look at him. "What? Are you kidding me? It took a sledgehammer for me to realize that I'd misjudged you. I'm so sorry I didn't have enough faith in you to talk to you. Can you forgive me? I expected the worst and didn't give you a fair chance."

I knew I was rambling, but I couldn't stop, so I continued, "I thought I'd dealt with the reality of my past—of a selfish and abusive and unfaithful ex-husband. I thought I was over it. But now I see why those dreams keep haunting me."

"Dreams? You mean you have nightmares about what he did to you?" Zave looked horrified.

"Yes. It's boiled down to the same degrading two-act-play over and over again. Maybe they'll stop now. But we can talk about that later. I'm so sorry for doubting you and shutting you out. I should have talked to you after that nasty run-in at the jewelry store."

Zave tilted his head to the side and squinted his eyes. "Jewelry store run-in? What was that?"

"Oh, we can talk about that later, too. It's another long, sneaky misunderstanding that includes Rhonda. I don't want to let Rhondas ever come between us ever again. I just want to hug you now and tell you I'm sorry I didn't give you a—"

Zave lowered his lips to mine. I forgot all the things I was sorry about and lost myself in his kiss…again.

"Uh hum." A cough interrupted my bliss.

"So it's true. You have the hots for the TV lady." Rhonda's voice sounded screechy.

We separated, reluctantly. Zave kept a protective arm around me.

I noticed Rhonda and the young man were now holding hands.

"Hello, Rhonda. Meet my girlfriend, Noelle Frost. Of course, you may have seen her before." Zave glared at her.

She remained silent. At least she had enough sense to lower her head as she stood there, caught in her deceit and nasty manipulations.

"Uh, hi, Triple X, I'm Bracken Trudeau. I'm a big fan." The young man stuck out his hand. He seemed to miss the tense atmosphere surrounding us.

Zave shook his hand, ever the gentleman. "Hello, Bracken. Nice to meet you. Where're you from?"

"University of Arizona. Junior year, thinking of jumping into the NBA early."

"Can I give you a bit of advice?" Zave asked him.

Rhonda was now looking all around the room, anywhere but at us.

"Sure." The young basketball player sounded eager.

"Stay in school. Finish your degree. Injuries are a way of life in the NBA and often cut careers short, but your degree will last you a lifetime," Zave said in a serious voice.

The young man looked crestfallen but thanked him and said he would think about it.

Rhonda yanked on his hand, and they left.

I turned toward Zave. He pulled me close.

"What you told that young man was certainly not what he wanted to hear. Great advice, though." I beamed up at him.

Zave nodded. "I try to tell it how it is. These young guys get stars in their eyes and want the money right away. I have seen too many of them come and go because of injuries. I hope he listens."

"You never cease to amaze me." I tapped his chin with my finger.

"I hope I can continue to amaze you for a long time, Elle." He lowered his lips to mine, and I was happily amazed once again.

Too soon, the kiss ended.

Zave whispered, lips close to my ear as he held me tight, "I thought I had lost you and Tatum. I've never given up on anything that I really cared about in all my life." His voice came out soft and ragged. "I just couldn't lose you two. I love you, Noelle Belle Frost. Would you and Tatum like to fly kites tomorrow?"

"Wait. What?" I leaned my head back to look him straight in the eye.

"I said, 'Would you and Tatum like to fly kites tomorrow?'" The right side of his mouth twitched.

"No. What did you say before that?" I wrapped my arms around his neck, thinking how great it was that I was tall enough to actually reach that far.

"Oh, just that I love you." He broke out into a full

smile. Then he leaned down and kissed me again.

The sweetest kiss I have ever known. In fact, it would go down in my memory as the honey kiss, it was so sweet.

His lips gently left mine and he said, "Well?" His eyes shone a dusky green, and his brows rose as he waited.

"Well, what?" My heart pounded as I paused. I knew what he wanted, but anticipation was half the fun.

"Do you love me, too?" The look on his face had changed to one of concern.

I teared up. My heart tried to beat out of my chest. Time had somehow stopped as I reached my hands up to cup both sides of his face. Then I whispered, "Xavier Maximillian Trayce, I love you."

Chapter Twenty

Today was not possible yesterday. Yesterday's today was dark and lonely, with a smile painted on. But today was a new day, thanks to the outlandish actions in front of the entire world by one man who had changed my universe, Xavier Maximillian Trayce, known to the sporting world as Triple X.

Zave and I stayed in the Nuggets Team box most of the night talking and kissing, then more talking and more delicious kissing. He dropped me off at the corporate condo a few hours before sunrise. I awoke to autumn sunshine coming through the window, and even more sunshine in my heart. Zave picked me up around nine, and we drove to Joy's to get Tatum.

At Joy's, Tatum ran to the door; ignoring me, she threw herself at Zave. She squealed in delight as he picked her up and swung her around in the air laughing his big belly laugh.

When they stopped spinning, she scolded him, "Now where have you been? I missed you." She gave him a kiss on the cheek, then hugged him tight.

"You're a charmer, like your mom, little lady," he said with a thick voice.

Tears, this time of happiness, sprinkled from my eyes. I looked over at Joy and saw that she, too, had watched the whole scene with tears in her eyes.

Before we left, Joy invited Zave to join us at the

Frost family Thanksgiving dinner at her house in a few weeks, raving about my incredible pies.

"Thank you, Joy," Zave answered humbly. "I would love to come, but I have games on the road the week of Thanksgiving."

He turned, still holding Tatum, and wrapped his arm around my shoulder. "Will you save me one of your pies?" he pleaded.

"Of course. The way you eat, I'll save you three or four." I grinned.

****

Zave and I took Tatum to gymnastics and sat in the parents' viewing gallery.

"She really is good for a five-year-old, Elle." Zave leaned forward with his elbows on his knees as he watched Tatum do a front walkover followed by a back bend into a kick-over. "Crazy limber, too," he added.

"She is. She has no fear and will try almost anything." I put my arm through Zave's. He sat up and scooted closer to me.

"She's that way with everything in life, isn't she?" Zave traced the lines in the palm of my hand.

"What did you say?" My hand tingled and burned at the same time.

He closed my hand in his and grinned. "Got to you, did I?"

I elbowed him and answered, "You wish."

Tatum bounded in with her pink gym bag slung over her shoulder and asked, "Did you see me, Tree? Did you see me do a flipper-doodle?"

"Oh, yeah, you were great! So that's a flipper-doodle, huh?" He gave her a high five. I could see he was fighting to keep a straight face.

"Yes, and I do good ones." Tatum beamed up at both of us.

"You sure do. Come on, my two beautiful ladies. It's time to fly kites."

We left the Olympic Training Facility amongst giggles and squeals of delight.

The rest of the day was remarkably simple and wonderful. Zave continued to be the perfect gentleman, kind and considerate of both Tatum and me. The wind was iffy, so sometimes our kites worked and other times…well, not so much. But it was okay. It was a lovely day, and all seemed right in our little corner of the world. Being all together felt comfortable. Three of us seemed a nice number. I realized it was good to have a man around after all—a nice man that is.

Chapter Twenty-One

Zave went on a road trip again for the next eight days. We talked every night, and much to my surprise, my nightmares stopped. What an incredible blessing and relief. My soul was truly healing from the abusive former marriage.

During one of those late and long phone calls, Zave and I finally had the chance to piece together the dreaded mock phone call by Rhonda. The one that had caused me to bolt that day at the jewelers.

Rhonda had staged it all. There wasn't anyone on the phone when she first approached me in my car with her over-the-top, sleazy "X, baby" talk. I realized when there was that little pause when she turned away from me and I shut my eyes, sick to death of what I was hearing, she must have used that time to press a pre-programmed button with Zave's number on it. Then pretended she was placing him on speakerphone from the prior fake call.

Zave told me he remembered the strange call from her a few weeks ago. After he'd said "Hello," Rhonda had greeted him with "X, baby, I have someone who wants to talk to you." He thought that was weird and had told her to hold on, he wanted to talk to her, but she ended the call quickly, telling him she'd call him back. He was going to tell her once again that he didn't have any feelings for her and to stop bothering him, which he did when she called him back again a few minutes later.

I told him what Rhonda had said when she was pretending to talk to him. The entire masquerade made sense now.

We both were stunned by how far she had been willing to go for her own purposes. This led into some great discussions on how to be prepared for odd situations in the future. First and foremost, we promised to always talk to each other and never trust outside situations, no matter how realistic they seemed.

Several times Zave stepped out while on a break during afternoon practices to call Tatum. I heard lots of giggles as she shared her school day with him. Each time he called, my admiration and appreciation for the man grew. Tatum was my world. No man could be welcome in it without room for her, too.

Zave had an early game on Thanksgiving. He made sure he called us at Joy's to wish us all a happy Thanksgiving. Joy and Holly had met him already, and Chrissy was chomping at the bit. I couldn't wait to introduce him to her when he returned home.

Each of my sisters brought enough food to feed an army. I'd baked ten pies, the usual ones: pumpkin, apple, cherry, and blueberry, chocolate cream, peach, and even a mincemeat—yuck. I also tried my hand at a praline pie. It was heavenly—now my new favorite.

Joy had invited Simon, but he had business out of town. I felt a little relieved. I still wasn't completely at peace with him. I shook it off as the reporter in me. Chrissy and Joy seemed to be ecstatic that he was back in our lives. It was Thanksgiving—time for me to be thankful for family—all my family.

It seemed that all of my sisters were more settled

than they had been for years. We ate, talked, and laughed a lot. Joy had invited Sean and his little boy. He was not only handsome but kind and seemed to truly love her and her boys. He certainly was patient with the craziness of our over-excited children bouncing around us all. I was happy for her.

Around the dinner table, we talked a lot about the upcoming groundbreaking for the new Nicholas Charles Frost Pediatric Wing at the Colorado Springs Hospital. Our parents had worked so hard for so many years; then after their deaths, we sisters had taken over the Frost Foundation, and the level-three pediatric wing was finally coming to fruition.

Joy said she had an important announcement. I looked at her finger—nothing. I had been so hopeful for her and Sean. Instead she shared that Mr. Arnett, our attorney for the Frost Foundation, had notified her that Simon had donated a substantial amount to the Frost Foundation.

Simon was turning out to be a blessing to our family, after all.

Chapter Twenty-Two

November thirtieth arrived with great anticipation. The day was always significant to the Frost sisters because it was our baby brother's birthday. But today was even more so. Today, we were holding the ground breaking of the Nicholas Charles Frost Pediatric Wing in his honor. I wished Zave could be there, but once again he had away games.

"Are you ready, sweetie? It's time to go." I held up Tatum's coat and helped her into it. The ground breaking was outside, of course, and although there wasn't any snow, it was cold and overcast.

My heart beat fast with excitement. This was a momentous occasion. A moment of sadness flitted through me as I thought of how my parents should have been with us today. They had worked hard for many years to secure the funds to make this day happen. After their car accident, we sisters continued their goal. It became every bit as important to us. A calm settled over me as I drove toward the hospital. My parents were here. They were proud. Somehow, I just knew it.

I smiled at Tatum in the rearview mirror as I pulled into the hospital parking lot. "We're here."

We hopped out of the warm car and into a cold breeze that blasted us from the top of the surrounding Rocky Mountains. Both Tatum and I pulled the collars of our coats up high around our necks as we made our way to the south side of the hospital, where chairs and an outdoor tent awaited us on the dirt field.

"Hi, Elle." Chrissy grinned at me, then added, "Hello, Miss Tatum," as she swooped her up into a big bear hug.

Tatum squealed with delight.

Chrissy gave her another squeeze before setting her down.

"Our seats are over here." Chrissy motioned to chairs on the front row, where Joy sat, trying to corral her three rambunctious boys.

A few moments later, Mr. Arnett, our attorney, who had helped our parents start the Frost Foundation years ago, shook each sister's hand and sat on the end of the front row to support us, almost like a surrogate father.

Chairs soon filled with local politicians and hospital administrators. I saw my TV station crew in the center of the mob and asked Chrissy to keep an eye on Tatum for a moment while I stepped back to say "hello" to them.

Normally, it would have been my story, since it was happening here in Colorado Springs, but because it involved my family, I couldn't cover it. After a reporter friend did a quick interview with me for a few soundbites, I hurried back to my seat.

My breath caught as I saw Simon arrive and saunter to the back row. Another cold breeze hit my face. I shivered, brushing aside any uncertain feelings about him. My research into Simon hadn't brought me any answers, good or bad.

I glanced at him again. Simon smiled at me. I returned the smile, thinking Chrissy was right. He looked so much like our father. A longing swept through me. I missed my parents, and I wanted Simon to be with us. After all, he did give a big donation to the Frost Foundation.

The chairman of the hospital board, Olivia Winn, stepped to the makeshift podium with a microphone. She welcomed everyone, spoke for a few minutes about the foundation, our parents' dedication, and shared a little about our family history, including sweet Nicholas.

From what I heard between helping keep Tatum and Joy's boys quiet, she spoke with sincerity and great appreciation.

There were shovels for each of us, including four small ones for our children. We made our way forward and lined up, facing the audience and the media. Tatum stood next to me, holding her shovel tightly. I got a lump in my throat, wishing my little brother had lived to have a childhood and the opportunity to grow up. He never even reached Tatum's age, and would have been in his late teens by now.

My sisters helped with Joy's boys. I assisted Tatum. Pictures flashed. I glanced up and saw red lights on most of the TV cameras. Cameras didn't bother me, but I hoped that Tatum and my nephews wouldn't choose now to become ninja warriors and start sword fighting with the shovels.

A tall, bald man in a gray coat interrupted our attempts to turn over a bit of frozen earth as he stepped through our line and announced he was looking for Mrs. Joy Frost Burton.

Joy raised her hand.

"Ms. Noelle Frost, Ms. Holly Frost, and Ms.

Christina Frost?" the man announced.

Each of us froze, confused, then nodded. After the man looked from one sister to another, he walked over to Joy.

"You are officially served," he said in a gravelly voice as he handed a packet of papers to her. Then he turned and scurried away.

Pandemonium broke out. The harsh wind picked up and swirled around us as we looked at each other, wondering what had just happened. The gray sky turned a darker shade of charcoal.

Joy shook her head as if to get her bearings, and then looked at the stack of papers in her hands as we circled around her.

Mr. Arnett joined us. Joy handed him the papers. We watched as he skimmed through the documents. "This looks like a legal stop-action. Ladies, please meet me at my office ASAP."

We looked at each other in confusion.

Mrs. Winn stepped over to us. "Everyone is getting cold. May we proceed?"

Mr. Arnett addressed the administrator. "May I make an announcement?"

She looked surprised but nodded.

Mr. Arnett walked to the podium. Clearing his throat and tugging at his collar, he spoke into the mic. "I'm Richard Arnett, attorney for the Frost Foundation. There has been a minor setback. We will be rescheduling the ground breaking. We are sorry for this inconvenience, folks. Please expect a press release in a day or two."

Stunned, everyone cleared out quietly.

I hurried out of the parking lot, drove away as

calmly as possible, and checked Tatum into school, much to her dismay. I promised we would do something fun that evening, since our day together had been interrupted.

My brain was reeling. This couldn't be real. There had to be some mistake. Our attorney would look over the documents, and it would all be fine.

I arrived as the secretary was ushering my sisters into Mr. Arnett's office. The mood was somber.

"What it comes down to, ladies, is the Frost Foundation's assets have been frozen." He took a moment to make eye contact with each of us before he continued. "Have you heard of Lyonstone, LLC?"

We all shook our heads.

"Neither have I. Lyonstone is claiming a share of the Frost Foundation's money. I'm afraid until we can work through this, construction on the new hospital wing will be delayed." He shook his head, a sad, hangdog look on his face.

The room spun as I clasped my hands and sank deeper into my seat. I heard several groans from my sisters. The attorney said something about taking a few minutes to get our thoughts together and stepped out of his office. We immediately formed a group hug, tears streaming. Deep inside, I knew we would make the hospital wing happen, someday, somehow.

Chapter Twenty-Three

When Zave called that evening after his game, I was still shaken up about the ground breaking fiasco and blurted out the whole awful story. It felt good to let it out, tears and all. He listened without interruption.

When I was finished, he cleared his throat and spoke softly. "I am so sorry, Elle. I think you're right. Your attorney will sort it out. It sounds like it's highly unlikely that this Lyonstone company has any rights to the Frost Foundation monies."

Then he said a generous "Zave thing." His financial manager had reviewed the Frost Foundation, and he was going to make a large donation. He also talked to the Nuggets' team owner and management. They thought it would be a great project to open up to other players and possibly even the team franchise.

I cut him off with "No, Zave, you can't ride in like a knight in shining armor and save us. We four sisters have to do this on our own. Plus, that would be taking advantage of our relationship, and I won't do that."

Somehow his offer made me panic. I never wanted to be in a position where I owed anybody, or another man had control over me. And I certainly didn't want to be rescued. We four sisters were strong. We could somehow make this work.

"Hold on, little lady. That's not what I meant. First, let me tell you that a donation from me is tax deductible and I'm always looking for tax deductions, so allowing me to donate to such a worthy cause is a win-win situation. Same with the franchise, or any other player. It would also make for good press."

"That sounds a bit crass." I was hurt. Press? Were they thinking of using our hospital wing to get big press?

"Elle, the Frost Foundation is a business. Hospitals are in the business of helping and healing people, but they are still a business. It's hard, but you need to take pride and emotions out of the business portion of the equation. Think about it. Those who donate large amounts to a cause usually need the tax break, but remember, they have a choice as to what charities they donate to. People prefer donating to something worthy, and that is how human nature works. Plus, it's not a bad thing to be recognized for doing something good."

When I didn't answer, Zave added, "I will hold off if it bothers you, but it could be a good back-up plan if you need it."

I started crying in earnest. Sobbing, in fact. I even snorted a time or two. Zave waited patiently for me to cry it all out. After a few minutes, I wiped the last of my tears and ended with a few hiccups.

"I wish I was there so I could hold you. You need some good hugs…and kisses."

That did the trick. I actually giggled like a schoolgirl into the phone. "Thanks for hearing me out. A dose of Zave is just what I needed tonight. I will think about what you said. I guess I'm all mixed up. This whole thing was such a shock." I stretched out on my bed, feeling more hope than I had since the bombshell of those horrible Lyonstone documents landed in our hands.

We visited for a while more. I must have been emotionally spent because I woke up several hours later with the phone still next to my ear. I had fallen asleep on Zave. I had never done that to anyone. It made me smile. I knew Zave wouldn't take it personally. In fact, I was sure he would be relieved that he was able to help me work through it enough to find some peace and sleep.

Chapter Twenty-Four

Today, December thirteenth, was my birthday, but since all of the Frost sisters' birthdays were in December, we usually celebrated together with a spa day. This year was no different. Zave was out of town with games again for a couple of days. He sent me a box of my favorite See's dark Bordeaux chocolates, and the most incredible, snuggly soft Denver-Nugget-blue, feather pillow with a note.

Happy birthday, Lovely Lady.
You and Tatum save me a few chocolates.
This pillow is so you can hug it instead of me while I'm away.
I love you,
Zave.

That night, as I waited for his call, I nestled into my birthday pillow and felt something hard. I looked closely at the pillow and saw an opening in the seam at one side. Reaching in, I found a box.

Hands trembling, I opened the box to find the most beautiful pastel-pink diamond surrounded with white diamonds, hanging on a rose gold chain. Taking it gently out, I watched the exquisite pale pink and white stones flash in the soft light from the lamp on my nightstand.

The phone rang.

"Happy birthday, Lovely Lady."

"Oh, thank you Zave. I found the necklace. It's absolutely gorgeous! Diamonds are my favorite, and pink ones are exquisite. You're spoiling me, for sure."

"Good, you deserve to be spoiled, and I want the job." I could hear the smile in his voice. This was better than a fairytale.

****

On Saturday afternoon before Christmas, there was a knock on the door. I peeked through the side window and saw a floral delivery truck out front.

I opened the door. A breeze of cold winter air chilled me to the bone within the first few seconds.

"Flowers for Ms. Noelle Frost and a Ms. Tatum Frost." A young man handed me two boxes. I grabbed my purple bag, gave him a tip, thanked him, and closed the door. I loved surprises.

"Tatum. Come here, sweetie. There's a surprise for us."

Tatum had been lying on the area rug watching *Scooby Doo*. She bounced into the dining room as I set the boxes on the table.

"Who's it from?" She bopped around with excitement.

"Hmm…" I read the label. "Zave, I mean Tree." I smiled at her. "Here, this one's for you. Shall we open them at the same time?"

She nodded.

"One, two, three!" we shouted as we pulled the stretchy gold strings off the boxes and lifted the lids.

I gasped. A bouquet of lovely baby pink roses, twenty-four of them, with one full-sized white rose in the middle which seemed to smile up at me.

Tatum bounced up and down as she clapped her

little hands. Her box held a bunch of yellow daisies.

I only needed to help her with "favorite" and "brighten" as she read her card by herself.

"To Tatum, my favorite little lady. These remind me of you. You brighten my day just because you are you. Love, Tree.

"They're so pretty, Mommy." She touched a petal softly.

"Zave's right. They remind me of you, too—pretty and happy." I gave her a big hug and then read my card out loud.

"To my favorite lady, I know you love baby pink roses...and...I love you. Love, Zave. P.S. Be ready for an adventure. Sometimes the best surprises are hidden in plain sight."

"Be ready for an adventure" and "surprises are hidden in plain sight" were nothing but riddles, and I was usually pretty good at riddles, but this time I had no clue. I'd ask him tonight when he called.

"Come on, my darling girl. Let's find a couple of vases from under the kitchen sink and get these lovely flowers in some water."

Tatum mimicked me and carefully picked up her flowers. We walked side by side to the kitchen. I let her help trim the stems before we placed each of our flowers one-by-one in the vases.

"Mommy?" Tatum paused and looked up at me, eyes wide. "Is Tree going to be my daddy?"

This could be a minefield. Not sure what to say, I fell back on the method of answering a question by asking a question. "Do you want him to be your daddy?"

"Well, Cassidy has a daddy and a mommy. Hunter

has a daddy, but no mommy. He says he wants one, and he still wishes you'd marry his dad, but I tolded him that you can't because Tree wouldn't like it." She rambled as she picked up another daisy, carefully snipped off an inch with her little scissors, and added it to her vase.

"Charlie and Micah and Mitchell have Aunt Joy, but, Mommy, they need a daddy, too." Tatum had puppy-dog eyes and sounded sad. Then within a flash, she cheered up and added, "I saw you kissing Tree, so now you have to marry him. He would be the awesomest daddy." She spoke as if it were a done deal.

I laughed. I liked her logic. Five-year-olds pretty much had life all figured out.

"You and I are a team, and we always will be. It's good to know that you're happy with us letting Tree on our team…if that happens." My voice trailed off. I thought of a future with Zave in it. My heart raced and warmth flooded my body from head to toe.

I wrapped my arms around my little girl and gave her a squeeze. Knowing that she wanted Zave in our lives made the situation somewhat simpler.

We spent the rest of the day cleaning the house, buying groceries, and having a picnic on a blanket while we watched more *Scooby Doo*. At bedtime, we said prayers, then snuggled on her bed for story time, our favorite time of the day.

She chose to read Cinderella. She could read most of the words herself. I laid my head by hers and listened to her sweet, sing-songy voice. I won the mother jackpot with such a wonderful little daughter.

My mind jumped back to the note delivered with the roses. "Be ready for an adventure." That could be fun. "Sometimes the best surprises are hidden in plain sight." Zave must have a special date planned for us.

"Mommy, what is this word?" Tatum snapped me out of my musings.

"Umm, it's 'cackled.' 'The stepmother cackled.' It's kind of a loud, annoying laugh that sounds like a chicken."

"Oh, okay," she continued to read. "The stepmother cackled, and then locked Cinderella in her attic bedroom. Cinderella sat on the floor and cried big tears. Two little mice climbed onto her lap. There was a knock at the front door. Mommy, there was a knock at the door." She tapped my shoulder.

"What?" I yawned. I must have dozed off.

"There's a knock at the door," Tatum said again.

"Uh-huh. Then it says, 'Cinderella looked out the attic window.' "

"Mommy. There's a knock at our door." She looked at me and giggled.

Sure enough, I heard a knock.

Who could be here this late? I hoped nothing was wrong with one of my sisters. A rush of alarm ran through my body, revving up for a possible emergency. I moved toward Tatum's bedroom window.

Tatum started to get up.

"No, honey, stay in bed," I cautioned her.

Moving the curtains aside, I saw a giant of a man— my giant of a man, standing on my front porch. My chest became a bell and my heart the chime bouncing around. "It's Tree."

She pushed her covers down.

"No, sweetie, it's past your bedtime. You can see him tomorrow. I'll leave the lamp on so you can read for a few more minutes, then go to sleep. I'll check on you in a little while." I kissed her on her forehead and headed downstairs, heart all twitter-pated.

Chapter Twenty-Five

I opened the door. He reached in and pulled me into his arms. "I missed you," he said as he hugged me, and then bent his head down to capture my lips with his. After a very thorough kiss, he lifted me up and carried me in, then settled on the couch with me in his lap. I giggled like a little schoolgirl.

"What are you doing here? I thought you weren't coming back until tomorrow night," I asked breathlessly as I looked at him with my arms encircling his neck. A whiff of fresh limes filled the air.

"I got the okay from Coach to fly in earlier than the team. Did you get the flowers I sent you and Tatum?"

"Yes. They're lovely! Tatum's, too. These are her first flowers. She felt so grown up." He watched my lips as I talked, then tipped his head down as if he needed another taste. After a few more moments of soft lips and silence, he pulled away slightly and looked at me. I could see the question in his eyes.

"What?" I asked him, confused.

"Are you sure you got my flowers? The tiny pink roses and one big white one?" his voice sounded anxious.

"Yes, I'm sure. They're in a vase on the kitchen table."

"Did you see the card?" His eyebrows pinched in.

"Yes, of course. I read it several times. I'll never

get enough of you telling me you love me." I paused to kiss his cheek and then added, "But I didn't have a clue about the rest of it. What adventure? And a hidden surprise in plain sight? I'm totally lost." I touched his forehead, trying to smooth the worry lines. At my touch, his face started to relax.

"May I see the flowers?"

"Uhh…yes." He was acting a little strange. The flowers were beautiful, but he seemed obsessed with them.

He stood up with me still cradled in his arms, then gently set me down. He took my hand as we walked into the kitchen.

"Here they are." I pulled them nearer to the edge of the table.

Zave bent over and looked at them closely. I watched as he removed the white rose. He held it close to his face and wiggled it around a little, then smiled.

Okay, this guy is almost certifiable—adorable and charming, but certifiable.

"Come with me." He gently took my hand again and led me back to the family room couch. I sat and then scooted over to make room for him. Instead, he handed me the white rose, then bent over the hearth and started a fire. Once the paper and wood caught, he knelt in front of me on one knee.

"Open it," he said quietly, his green eyes midnight-moss colored in the soft light.

I looked at the rose. "Open the rose?"

"Uh-huh." He nodded his head.

I shrugged and said, "All righty, then," my sharp vocabulary rising to the challenge. I carefully pulled the petals apart. The light from the fire flashed. I stopped and looked up at him. The expression on his face was one of sheer anticipation, as if he were a boy expecting his first basketball.

"What do you see?" he asked with excitement.

I looked back at the rose. As I pulled another petal away from the center, I gasped. There, nestled deep in the rose, was a ring. Not just any ring, but a ring that sparkled white and pink.

With shaking hands, I lifted it out and held it up close to my face, dumbfounded. It was the most beautiful ring I'd ever seen. A large, white, oval diamond sat in the center, surrounded by smaller pink diamonds. More pink diamonds, this time bevel-set, ran down both sides of the band made of pink gold. The light of the fire danced off the diamonds as I held it out in front of my face.

I quivered with excitement, and the ring seemed to glow.

Zave grinned wide, then readjusted his knee as if to brace himself. He cupped my face with his hands and kissed me butterfly soft.

"Sweetheart, I'm willing to keep proving to you for the rest of my life that I'm a good guy and will always treat you with kindness and respect—Tatum, too. I promise to always have integrity and never betray our love...Noelle Belle Frost...will you marry me? Forever?" He looked deep into my eyes. His eyes seemed to sparkle bright green.

Tears streamed down my face. "Yes."

Zave gently took the ring from my shaking hand and slid it onto my fourth finger on my left hand.

He leaned over and wrapped his arms around me, pulling me up as he stood. His kiss was soft at first, then deeper. My entire body tingled. This was more than a honey kiss—it was a crème brulée kiss—the sweetest, most lovely of kisses. I realized then and there that I was in for a delectable feast of kisses from now on.

Footsteps interrupted us.

Tatum jumped into our arms, breaking up that most delicious kiss of all time as she sang, "We're getting married. We're getting married!"

Zave lifted me up, too, and spun us in circles as we all sang, "We're getting married. We're getting married. We're getting married…"

This was going to be the best Christmas ever. Zave's love had opened up a healing door for me. He had unlocked my heart and my soul.

All three of us laughed as Zave put us down.

Tatum looked up and asked, "Can we get married on Christmas?"

Zave looked at me.

"That's pretty quick to pull a wedding together. How about if we wait until the next holiday—Valentines?" I joked.

"Oh, yes!" Tatum squealed.

"Perfect, and you two lovely ladies can be my Valentines," Zave agreed.

"And you're our Christmas miracle." I smiled back at him, just before he bent over and gave Tatum a kiss on her forehead. Then he gave me another delicious kiss. This one was a Christmas sugar plum kiss.

To continue the story of the Frost sisters with the third book of the series, look for...

Holly's Heart

by

Melinda Sanchez

Here's how it begins:

Chapter One

Tiny sparkles in the tile reflected light in the dim hallway as I passed between rooms. Numerous vital checks and a dozen doses of medicine later, I welcomed a ten-minute break before I tackled the paperwork—mounds and mounds of paperwork.

The door to the employee lounge expelled a soft gush of air as I entered, looking to quiet my hunger pangs with a stale treat from the vending machine. I peered closely to choose between an apple and a strawberry granola bar, and someone came up from behind and poked me in the ribs. I let out a squeal and spun around to the laughing face of my co-worker, Alice. We cupped our hands over our mouths. If we woke the patients at three o'clock in the morning, we would spend the next several hours getting them all settled again.

"What are you thinking? You'll get us both fired," I whispered.

Alice stood half a head shorter than me and her curls bobbed as she stifled her giggle. "You almost jumped a mile."

"You almost gave me a heart attack."

"Well, you are in the right place for it, anyway. But what are you doing working another night shift, Holly? You work more overtime and late shifts than any nurse I know. You have seniority, you know."

"There's such a high demand in pediatrics. They needed someone."

"Ehh—like I said, you are covering for this shift too much. Maybe you need someone, Holly. Someone at home you don't want to leave at night."

I smiled. "My cat? Oh, she's fine. But seriously, sometimes I want to be here late like this."

"Yeah, right." She smirked.

"I do, especially here in pediatrics. The empty quiet is too spooky for some of these kids. Their little whispery voices and soft, pudgy hands get to me. I like giving comfort in the middle of their lonely nights."

Alice and I both looked over in surprise when someone sat up on the couch in the back of the lounge.

"You need a man, honey. Good—bad—it don't matter, as long as it's a man."

I looked into the plump face and dark eyes of our

nurse's aide, Mrs. Torres, and put my hands on my hips. "I've got people sneaking up on me all over in this place. I didn't know it would be so scary in here."

She shook her head. "No, honey, you need to hear what I say. You want to give comfort so much? That means you need comfort. You need a man."

I cleared my throat and pushed the hair that had come loose from my ponytail back behind my ear. "Ha. Well, you may be right. But nowadays I wonder if I'd be better off to forget men altogether."

Her eyes narrowed, and she pursed her lips. "Oh dear, you got it worse than I feared. You are in love with a man who breaks your heart." She wiggled to her feet. "I've been an aide here a long, long time, and I seen you come and go, come and go all the time. You are too lonely, Miss Holly."

My words froze for a moment before I opened my mouth to protest again, sure that I'd given her the wrong impression. But she walked up shaking her head and waved her hand in front of my face to shush me.

"You stare in space with those big eyes like that; I know what I see." She scribbled something on the back of a patient's menu card someone had left on the coffee table and handed it back to me. "Here is my number. My Pablo is not married. He is going bald and is a little lazy, but he has a good heart."

The breakroom door closed behind Mrs. Torres when she left, and Alice and I had our hands over our mouths again, stifling a laugh.

"I didn't know I was so transparent," I whispered.

Alice's eyes widened before she headed out of the lounge. "You better watch out; Pablo may show up during your shift with a bouquet of roses one of these days."

I laughed and shook my head before I turned back to the vending machine. Mrs. Torres loved to mother the young nurses, but at age twenty-eight, I'd certainly learned a few things about my own life and knew my own feelings. There was no way I was "transparent" because of a broken heart. Those days were long gone, sewn up and tossed, wrapped and buried, resolved and finished. *Fini*, as I'd learned to say in France last year.

I chose the strawberry granola bar and washed it down with bottled water. It hit my stomach in a lump.

A word about the author...

Cindy R. Williams, a born storyteller, grew up in Utah, surrounded by lilacs and creating magical worlds with her big sister and little brother. She had aspirations of becoming a mermaid and imagines mystic lands where good prevails and all are safe and free.

Cindy took time out of her magical world to graduate Brigham Young University. In her years on this planet, she has been a state gymnast, a lifeguard, in an all-girl rock band called Fancy Hardware, the Membership Director of KBYU-TV, a professional harpist and a teacher of guitar, ukulele, piano, and harp. She is a member of ANWA, American Night Writers Association.

Cindy's greatest accomplishments so far are mothering five remarkable human beings and grand-mothering eight adorable tornadoes.

These days she lives in the Sonoran Desert with her handsome husband, a pug, two silly cats, two water frogs, and thirty-six guppies. She is completing one of her major bucket list items—writing and sharing her stories. Cindy writes for a statewide newspaper, has five books published, numerous stories in anthologies, and her fifty-plus adventures floating on her computer.

http://cindyRwilliams.com